13 LIVES

13 LIVES

Stories of Others

Michael Pawlowski

| N₁ | O₂ | N₁

CANADA

Library and Archives Canada Cataloguing in Publication

Pawlowski, Michael, 1949–
[Short stories. Selections]
13 lives : stories of others / Michael Pawlowski.

ISBN 978–1–988098–45–6 (softcover)

I. Title. II. Title: Thirteen lives.

PS8631.A925A6 2018   C813'.6   C2018–900457–6

Printed and bound in Canada on 100% recycled paper.

Now Or Never Publishing
901, 163 Street
Surrey, British Columbia
Canada V4A 9T8

nonpublishing.com
Fighting Words.

We gratefully acknowledge the support of the Canada Council for the Arts
and the British Columbia Arts Council for our publishing program.

To
Alicia Verdi
for her support and inspiration
and to
All
who have a respect
for the infinite grandeur of God's creation

13 Lives

Prologue

"Become the person you want your neighbour to be." Chief Clifford's instruction in 1961 was my introduction to native culture with all of its tribulations, dreams and achievements.

13 Lives recounts events in the lives of thirteen individuals from the respectfully proud chief to the poor soul alone in his hour of his need. More than forty years in public service has provided opportunities to meet and befriend these persons. They are not all celebrated. They are not all impoverished. In recording 'the rest of the story' a sincere attempt is made to dispel preconceived notions that have generated stereotypical views of indigenous persons. No one benefits from predetermined opinions.

13 Lives records actual events with real persons. Some names have been amended to protect the identity of the person, family or community. This is necessary as some of the narratives include minors or suggestions of less than appropriate actions within a native community. There are no fabricated stories, although some are endowed with literary liberties.

The author appreciates the efforts of those assisting the First Nations. This group includes a lawyer and two clerics.

The stories of indigenous persons include the abused, the homeless, the suicidal, those seeking a world away from the reserve, and those returning to the native community to perfect themselves. In all of these narratives, nature is so very much an intricate aspect of their lives.

We commemorate their struggles and celebrate their success knowing that they now or in the future will rejoice in timeless Wisdom, Truth, Honesty, Respect and Love within the Eternal Realm of the Great Spirit.

I

CLIFFORD

Moccasins gripped the logs, his toes recognizing every node. Slowly he eased across the makeshift shoreline, that had become permanent with time, to eventually stop at the southern expanse. There he looked up with ardent appreciation, his gaze absorbing the cresting waters as they rapidly followed the wind towards the northern basin. Beyond the lake there were trees: tall pines, birch and maple. Even the mist could not obscure their grandeur on that August morning. Curve Lake, he called the expanse of fresh water, being ever so thankful for the sustenance it shared. Others, especially seasonal visitors, called it Chemong Lake. Other lakes all had their own identity but truly remained part of the same aquatic environs his people called 'home'.

Clifford's gaze remained fixed to the southeast. How many times had he paddled those waters? Fourteen kilometers was the distance south to Fowler's Corners. Before that he would occasionally stop at Bridgenorth. Shaking his head, he again smiled, grateful for every moment in such creative opulence.

His trek returning more than a kilometer along the shore to his cabin was slow and meditative. Each step was deliberate as if declaring his praise to the many who had walked that path for centuries. "Each native person shares a universal spirit in the goodness and grandeur of creation." Clifford had recited that phrase often as if declaring the foundation of his spiritual practice. He always felt close to God, and his ancestral heritage ensured that relationship.

Being fluent in English with some ability in French provided him with additional opportunities to espouse his philosophy. He never had the opportunity to complete grade school. On his own he acquired the understanding of other languages and dialects: Ojibwa, various phrases in Mohawk, and all of the tongues and expressions common to the proximate First Nations. These were an assembly born out of treaties, the resolution of land claims, and more importantly a similar celebration of life. The First Nations of Curve Lake, the Hiawatha, Alderville and the Mississaugas of Scugog pursued harmony while remaining distinct. They shared similar creation stories and conveyed sincere interest in the other narratives of native lore.

These communities were all part of an ancestral domain called Anishinaabe that included portions of present-day Quebec, Ontario, New York, Michigan, Ohio and Wisconsin. The tribes included the Odawa, Potawatomi, Algonquin, Delaware, Mississauga, and the Ojibwa. Together they shared their belief in the Great Spirit.

Clifford was born about ten years after the first recitation of Chief Yellow Hawk's universal prayer for peace in the 1880s. He recited it daily, being more devoted to that practice than any Christian's commitment to say the Our Father.

O Great Spirit, whose voice I hear in the winds and whose breath gives life to all the world, hear me. I come before you, one of your children. I am small and weak. I need your strength and wisdom. Let me walk in beauty and make my eyes ever behold the red and pur-ple sunset. Make my hands respect the things you have made, my ears sharp to hear your voice. Make me wise, so that I may know the things you have taught my peo-ple,the lessons you have hidden in every leaf and rock. I seek strength, not to be superior to my brothers, but to be able to fight my greatest enemy: myself. Make me ever ready to come to you with clean hands and straight eyes, so that when life fades as a fading sunset, my spirit may come to you without shame.

To the white man the seventh decade was anticipated as a time of peace and prosperity. Their war was over. Jobs were plentiful. Technology seemed to have no limits. Their President had even pledged to put a man on the moon, a task that seemed so improbable. Yet it was an age of fear. Prior generations had never heard the term 'nuclear'. Diplomacy had become a display of threat. Though many concluded this was a wonderful time to be alive, Clifford had reasons to be cautious.

As he eased along the path appreciating the call of various birds and the scurrying of adventurous chipmunks into the brush, Clifford smiled to himself. Still, it was a wry expression reflecting dual personalities: one thankful and the other dismayed. He was learned in spite of his limited education. More than most, he considered the past when assessing potential consequences. That day he knew was special to some and for others it was a guilty verdict. August 3, 1961 was the 90TH anniversary of the treaty declaring:

> Your Great Mother, therefore, will lay aside for you land to be used by you and your children forever. She will not allow the white man to intrude upon these lots. She will make rules to keep them for you, so that as long as the sun shall shine, there shall be no Indian who has not a place that he can call his home, where he can go and pitch his camp or if he chooses to build his house and till his land.

A moment of silence stopped him just before a patch of raspberry bushes void of their berries. A deep sign followed with recollection of mistreatment and tribulation bordering on the criminal.

"We're so prone in Canada to condemn the States," he thought to himself when once again pondering the mistreatment north of the border. In the Canadian provinces the treachery had become a prolonged systematic approach to demeaning people who were proud of their native ancestral heritage.

In 1874, three years after a seemingly magnanimous accord granting entitlement to ownership of land, the federal government guaranteed the inferior status of tribal members by confining them to reserves and making them wards of the state. To Clifford it had always been abhorrent for the Canadian government to refer to itself as "She" as if Ottawa had adopted these many tribes as their mother.

The Residential Schools began in 1884. They were state-funded and operated by religious denominations. Within twenty-one years there were more than one hundred such schools in the country.

Those English and French speaking citizens, relaxing comfortably on their estates, knew that conditions were pathetic for the native people. In 1907 Dr. Bryce, who was an inspector with the Department of Indian Affairs, reported on the wretched health conditions on the reserves. He even called the lack of care "criminal." Three years were spent dismissing his report.

"The final solution to the Indian Problem" was the government's legislation in 1910 in which contractual obligations were established with those religions operating the Residential Schools.

In 1919, the death rate from tuberculosis in the Residential Schools was approximately seventy-five percent. In spite of this, the government abolished the post of Medical Inspector for Indian Residential Schools.

As if totally disregarding these deaths, during the next year the federal government decreed that upon reaching age seven, every native child had to attend a Residential School. Children were sent to their death. In spite of this, to this day Canada enshrines the image of that Prime Minister on its $100 bill.

The province of Alberta in 1928 instituted the forced sterilization program. More than three thousand native women were sterilized in that province. The plan was also considered in other regions.

Throughout the 1930s there were reports across the country that herds were being hunted to extinction. Residents on some reserves starved to death.

During the height of the Great Depression, the principals of Residential Schools were made the legal guardians of all native students. The native parents were forced to surrender their children to the custody of the school's principal.

In the 1940s studies confirmed that malnutrition was a major issue on the reserves. Yet nothing positive happened. Meanwhile the Prime Minister in Ottawa was fascinated with his ability to see ghosts and hear strange voices.

Immediately following World War Two, the Canadian government allowed the American CIA to conduct medical, biological and psychological tests on native children. As abhorrent as that was, the CIA was employing the services of ex-Nazi researchers to complete the tests. The Gulags of the Soviet Union had come to Canada.

In 1951 an Amendment to the Indian Act allowed for the consumption of alcohol on the reserves. The stereotypical image of the native was preserved.

It wasn't until 1960 that natives were given the right to vote.

Then, in 1961, an entity called the National Indian Council was established to represent the treaty and status natives, a group called 'non-status Indians', and the Métis aboriginals. The Council refused to represent the Inuit. Perhaps the government felt it was advantageous to divide aboriginal interests.

Clifford had lived through all this. Though he was proud, he also felt shamed that he survived and to that day was looked upon with some respect in the Curve Lake First Nation. He returned to the water's edge looking beyond the expanse of white caps and then venturing his gaze towards the basin. For those moments he stared intently recognizing every stump as it interrupted the flow of waves, and each patch of weeds that supported his income. There was peace in that lake, where all of the tribulations of the world were washed away with the excitement of that large catch.

The drizzle started once again and with it the fog started to sweep across the lake. This was not uncommon. Moments later it could be bright and sunny once again. Moving from the shore, his feet guided him instinctively along the path as quickly as they could go in the direction of his cabin. He didn't run, nor was it a pace. His right foot caused him to limp occasionally, but at the same time it became a fulcrum to thrust his left leg in the intended direction.

Normally he would have stopped to inspect the dock. He did that daily mainly for something to do. The complex was securely imbedded deep into the clay base to prevent shifting and winter damage. The three flags blew proudly above the terrain displaying his allegiance: the Canadian Ensign, the Stars and Stripes and the Ojibwa Insignia.

The fire he had lit before leaving the cabin, thus the three-room convenient structure was already warm. The afternoon would naturally be warm, but mornings were always a trifle cool. Removing his tunic, he pondered the generic term 'weather'. He deplored its use when others would curse various forms of precipitation or the wind. Clifford firmly believed no one could ever ascribe just one word to the many facets of the Creator's fascinating gift. Other terms regarding inclement conditions also puzzled him. "What do they expect in winter?"

Then, rising, he prepared himself a cup of herbal tea using the old kettle on the potbelly stove. He had electricity but that was a luxury reserved for company. If he wanted to be one with the creator he had to use what the creator gave him. "Actually," he thought, "the kettle's probably just as old."

Across the lake the twelve-year-old rowed his wooden boat back to shore. The vessel was indeed an antique. They had stopped making these boats that size, out of wood, about five years before. Of course a local company was still making wooden motor boats, but the smaller ones had been replaced by metal versions. The youth preferred the wooden structure because fish didn't make so much noise when flopping around. Actually there weren't many fish caught that morning. The first day in the rented cottage gave him ample time to fish. He caught more then. But this, the second day, maybe the fish went elsewhere, especially the pickerel.

The lake was so peaceful even with the choppy water. It was solitude. He never understood why but grade six had been so stressful. Was he just growing up? Was he feeling alone being an only child? Or, was it just having nothing to do? He's wasn't good at hockey because of his weak ankles. He was never selected for the soccer team. He could run, but that didn't get him anywhere.

Fortunately he could play baseball and always made the school team. Third base was his role—the position where errors were forever remembered. However that season was so short. More recently in terms of baseball, he was still excited by the two All Star Games. There were two that year: one in San Francisco and the other in Boston. The last was just four days ago on the 31ST of July. Don't bother to ask him about his favourite player. The answer would always involve many possibilities: Musial, Mays, Mantle, Yastrzemski, Gibson, Ford, Maris, Aaron, Robinson or Cepeda.

Fishing, as simple and mundane as any sport could be, gave him that extra sense of importance. After reaching his limit that he always set at four, he mastered catch-and-return. Yes, there were perpetually annoying moments when the same sunfish would be on the hook seconds later.

It was hard to distinguish aspects of the distant shore. It was generally a dark mass with the sun highlighting the tree tops. The mist and drizzle of course didn't help perception of anything that far away. His parents had arranged, with the impetus of the resort owner, to visit a native chief that evening. The information was not always consistent or thorough as to what to expect on the other side of the lake. There were festivities scheduled for the second week of their stay, and they had already arranged to visit the reserve on Buckhorn Lake on that occasion.

The youth that was in that boat is the author. This narrative is the recollection of four visits with the native chief, the visit to the reserve and a subsequent visit to the Paudash area. Opportunities presented themselves to visit historical settings and converse with many who were acquainted with the persons and circumstances involved. For these nameless many, sincere gratitude is expressed.

We arrived at Clifford's cottage just before 8PM that evening. With the sun setting in approximately forty minutes' time we had at least crossed the lake in daylight. Taking the motor boat home across the lake in the dark would present a greater peril. However we left enough lights on in our cabin to provide sufficient direction. When we arrived, "the Chief" was still out on the lake. That was the respectful title we were to call him, much like university students perpetually calling an ex-coach by the title he once bore. The dock was easily accessible with enough bolts to fasten the ropes. The property was well-landscaped. His cottage within the trees was still aglow with some sunlight highlighting the cedar stain. His cats greeted us with a series of expectant meows. We waited for his arrival.

He was there within twenty minutes. His guests outnumbered the muskies they had hoped to catch. Actually there were three guests and no fish. First impressions always count. He appeared a happy person. His attire was not that of a person one would usually call 'chief'. His brown corduroy pants were partially hidden by a long sleeve tunic that was secured by a red cloth belt. The colours of the TPTs decorated his cap. The Toronto-Peterborough-Transit company was an ardent supporter of minor league sports in the Peterborough area.

Inside the cabin we were introduced to the three gentlemen from Texas. Their drawl made the evening fascinating. I truly wondered how these three and the chief understood each other. Clifford spoke in a harsh voice, somewhat unexpected for a person his age. The conversation quickly became lively. Initially it concentrated on fishing which is the reason they were visiting and why they had hired the chief. Clifford showed us an old wooden lure that he had used to catch a muskie that he claimed exceeded fifty pounds. It was absolutely amazing to see: the handmade wooden wedge about eight inches long pierced with wire hooks sticking out of all sides. The original ocher colour was barely discernible. He held it proudly smiling at his accomplishment.

Normally he would take his guests out early in the morning or about five in the afternoon. Their late arrival delayed the events on the initial day. There were plans to be there by six the next morning. However, they seemed very much prepared to take as much time as necessary to listen to his tales.

It was our questions that prompted his information. Responding to the initial series, Clifford extrapolated on his past. This was a tale of tragedy.

Clifford grew up on the reserve, and attended a Residential School. Even though he was abused, he dismissed it at the time as his punishment was far less than that inflicted upon others.

In World War One he fought at the Somme. Because of his race, he was not sent to the front line or even to the trenches initially. Whether they could not be trusted, he could only surmise. Vividly he commented on the corporals and sergeants and their inability to adequately lead. Whatever he and his compatriots suggested was dismissed, which might have been the reason they were initially kept away from the battle. Clifford survived the typhus that devastated Europe after the war. However, he confessed he must have been a carrier of the disease as his wife died within weeks after his return.

In the 1920s he was actively involved in building roads and digging wells. Ottawa then promised assistance maintaining the roads but didn't have a snow plow available. Disappointments were directly proportional to his disputes with the government. It was all the federal government's task at that time, which made it easy for provincial politicians and municipal councillors to just refer him elsewhere.

He deplored the lack of adequate education and training, suggesting that it was definitely, "the government's means to make sure we stayed put." Clifford struggled with the entire program of Residential Schools. Proudly he declared that eventually he was able to have input regarding the teachers in the regional school.

Throughout, the tourists from Texas were attentive. Assuredly they were wondering how all this could happen. Clifford never asked them about the Sioux, Anasazi, Pawnee, Comanche and other tribes.

The Texans landed their Muskellunge the next morning. Depending on whom you talked to determined its size and weight. It was caught just to the north of the second most prodigious patch of weeds. Such a spot was usually the home for smaller fish and ducklings.

That second night I returned to Clifford's cabin with my father. My mom had had enough fish stories. The whole context of the discussion was the chief's childhood, especially the poverty, lack of proper schooling, and nutrition that didn't meet third world standards.

After I asked, "What is it like in winter?" we received a detailed description of life with limited food supplies, roads buried in snow, and the only means of survival to cross the lake—all of its one kilometer width—amid ice flows for the convenience store. The vendor was there to assist the natives but was clearly positioned on white-man's land to be accessible to white-men if they ever chose not to buy from their preferred outlets.

When the chief handed me a small wooden tomahawk the conversation turned to arts and crafts. Clifford was skilled in whittling. His wife had majored in weaving blankets. Others within the Curve Lake First Nation were adept in a full range of souvenirs including pottery, handbags, clothing, purses, rugs, sweaters, and carvings.

It was during my fourth visit, during the day, after our Texan friends had left, that Clifford talked about his time as Chief. He was proud of how much he had done because it equalled all that he could possibly have achieved with the limited resources available and the federal government's unfulfilled promises. He then spent more than two hours telling various creation stories, and recounting aboriginal lore.

We parted company after that. Here was a gentleman committed to every aspect that made this world a wonderful place. He was serious, and yet hopeful. The Chief was appreciative of a good listener, and had an incredible ability to keep his audience attentive. He obviously cared about his First Nation with such concern that would never fade with the sunset.

To get to the pow-wow the following Tuesday, we had to steer our boat across Chemong Lake, and then through the channel to Buckhorn Lake. The setting for the festivities on the Curve Lake First Nation was their main meeting grounds on the eastern shore of Buckhorn Lake. Clifford would be able to attend on foot if he just followed the paths through the forest. However he had no plans to be there that day.

The activities matched our expectations: tribal dancing, chanting, drums and decorative headdresses. The arts and crafts attracted significant attention. One woman in particular knitted winter jackets in which the interior was also stitched, securing between the two layers a piece of animal skin for thorough protection. Her items sold fast. Wooden carvings too were in much demand. Decorative clay pots were similarly selling for reasonable prices. The major attraction was the raffle for a 1950 Chev. The residents could not believe their good fortune when one of them won the car. After two hours we were ready to leave. It was then that we discovered that someone had cut the rope and stole our anchor. How could they? Why would they? It was just a tin can filled with cement.

After my parents passed away, forty-two years following my only visit to that lake, I attended the Paudash Community. In the course of my visit, I met several elders and natives at a café. We talked for hours. They initially expressed their disappointment with recurring "False Promises." Their explanation provided ample reason for them to feel such betrayal.

An elderly native, with a rough beard, the one who appeared to be most respected in the group, started his narrative referring to the "White Paper by that Frenchman." He was specifically referring to the Trudeau government in 1969 and the recommendation of Jean Chrétien who, as the Minister of Indian Affairs, wished to abolish the Indian Act. That in effect put an end to the federal government's domain over native matters. Those responsibilities were being distributed mainly to the provincial governments who in turn could assign many departments to do the same task or delegate the authority to regional or municipal authorities or even to a First Nation community. All of those changes muddled the care and education available to the aboriginal communities.

Another aboriginal gentleman, who was far less vocal than the first, mentioned Elsie Knott. His explanation enlightened me, or at least gave me basic opinionated information. She had been elected Chief of the Curve Lake First Nation in 1954, the first woman in Canada to hold that position. The views on her leadership were varied. Most agreed some good was accomplished. Two persons who did not belong to the Curve Lake tribe questioned the idea of a woman being Chief. The elder gentleman with the rough beard silenced his tribal brothers, reminding them that she was beneficial to her tribe in her efforts and achievements.

Other comments about another woman followed. They identified her as Ellen Fairclough. I listened intently as once again the opinions significantly differed. She was the first woman cabinet minister, an appointment by Mr. Diefenbaker in May of 1958. Her portfolio was Citizenship and Immigration. That alone caused many in the café to challenge the real intent of the federal government. Aboriginal issues were in her domain solely because they had been included under the concept of Citizenship. Instead of seriously addressing the dire poverty and travesty on the reserves, Ms. Fairclough proposed and advocated the concept of women's rights, particularly equal pay. This was a woman who had belonged to the United Empire Loyalists and the Zonta Club, whose groups rarely addressed the conditions in the First Nations. She could have done more if she was adequately prepared. That was the consensus in the café that day.

Then they responded to my queries regarding Clifford. It was obvious that he was respected beyond the realm of the Curve Lake First Nation. They recounted his efforts while he was that nation's Chief in the 1940s. It was also noted that no one ever heard Chief Clifford speak ill of any woman. They praised his efforts regarding roads and transportation, health and fresh water, care for the seniors and access to the local hospital. It was also mentioned that decisions and conditions affecting natives elsewhere did not control events at Curve Lake. The litany was incredible. They described a tough negotiator, a fierce competitor, and a man who would never jump before considering all of the consequences. They talked again of his leadership and his attempts to enhance the perception of the native. Then a younger native gladly mentioned the plans at Trent University to offer courses in native studies. He had little information, but was very proud of the impetus to record their ancestral heritage.

Another mentioned their own cemetery. That seemed so basic.

The elderly gentleman then talked about the Whetung Ojibwa Centre and its influence as a venue for tourism and information.

They conveyed their pride, some enthusiasm and many dreams. Life would go on and they pledged to do what they could to make it better not just for themselves but for generations to come. As I left the Paudash Community that Saturday afternoon, I was very mindful of the overall impact Clifford had had on his Curve Lake Community.

Perhaps the impact of Chief Clifford and his native community were never truly recognized until June, 2016 when the current Chief of the Curve Lake First Nation was called upon to represent all aboriginal nations in declaring respect for Muhammad Ali in front of tens of millions of viewers at the prize fighter's funeral.

2

AMELIA

Backstage the adulation resounded. The thirteen-year-old still attired in her white cassock extinguished her flickering candle while the audience continued its enthusiastic applause. Fellow classmates and friends had all expected as much. An aura of grateful satisfaction emanated from the corridors. She had nailed the talent show's penultimate performance, "Let There Be Peace on Earth". The composer, Jill Jackson Miller, would have been most impressed.

For the finale, Amelia joined the entire junior choir singing the inspirational song, "I Believe". Ardently the audience shared their voices with the meaningful lyrics. Her expression continued to capture the hearts of several thousand parishioners.

Each year, that Catholic parish in North End Toronto staged a production entertaining the interests of seniors while delighting the youth. Impromptu comedy, skits, and musicals generated applause in the prior four years. The "Mikado" had been a thorough success blending the props with appealing melodies. "My Fair Lady" had been endearing. Each year was a challenge to improve upon the past. In 1962, the director chose to highlight the abilities of the parishioners themselves in performances destined to display their talents. The entire show was discussed within parish groups for months thereafter.

Amelia left with her parents immediately after the final encore. It was almost midnight. She adored family life in all of its components. Her parents were the best. However, every child thought that in the age before the commonality of divorce. She was never one to boast or assert superiority. Appreciation for everything was never expressed publicly, but in her prayers gratitude was always first to be mentioned. Her perception of her God embraced every aspect of nature. It seemed to simplify everything: each decision, the difficulties in life, and those moments of unexpected joy. Her God was the Supreme Being, the Catholic Deity with the Trinity. She adored Christ's love and the Blessed Virgin Mary's desire to be an intercessor in her life. Yet, she also found her God in the joy of friendship, the companionship of adoring pets, the kind expressions of neighbours, and the efforts of many whose names she never knew. Her God could be found in the nature trails, athletic ventures, or quiet moments in the park. Amelia was truly the epitome of being 'a good Christian girl'.

Her appearance certainly generated that impression. At five feet four inches, she carried herself resolutely among friends and acquaintances. Her ash-blonde hair she always kept short. Only on one occasion did it ever touch her shoulders. Her expression seemed to penetrate anyone with whom she would converse, as if reading the heart as well as the mind. Words were an expression of the soul, a means of conveying purity, effort and determination. She had trouble at times finding just the right expression. Being bilingual was an asset, even though academic studies were solely in English. French was her heritage. She was well aware of the benefit, yet also how distinct she was.

Her parents were devout Catholics and seemed perpetually happy. There were only a few instances of frustration in front of the children. They had met and married in Saint-Jerome, about thirty miles north-west of Montreal. Her father in his youth had worked with a logging company. Amelia understood that that was somewhere closer to Hudson's Bay. Somehow, just after his twentieth birthday, he was able to secure a position with the provincial tourism agency working within a lodge. That was definitely good fortune. In 1944, Hydro-Quebec, having just been formed that year, created thousands of jobs affecting prosperity in related and divergent industries. Tourism was one. His position never directly involved attending the visitors' needs. Rather, his job was multifaceted, being general maintenance for every possible situation within the complex. In that venue, he met the young lady who would be Amelia's mom.

They worked together there, and then moved to Montreal. Amelia was born there in early February, just days after the province adopted its new flag in 1948.

In spite of industrial expansion, the politics of Quebec following the war created an unstable situation. Maurice Duplessis returned to power with The Union Nationale in 1944 and then repeated his victory in 1948. That economic situation basically forced her parents to move to Toronto. In Ontario, he found work as a machinist using his acquired skills. Amelia's mother, after a long search, obtained employment with a French Canadian life insurance company on Bay Street.

Amelia was the eldest of three children. Her sister was born just more than a year later. They had, at the time, already settled in southern Ontario. Their brother came into the world three years later. The family had a pet dog. She called it a 'Heinz 57 terrier'. Amelia loved its affection, but ultimately when her brother started being more active and independent, the family pet latched onto him for the attention and activity it instinctively desired.

Nothing much was ever said during her early years about her grandparents. She never knew them. Names were mentioned only on special occasions in the company of friends. She had an uncle, her mother's brother, in Quebec who had more information about the rest of family. Amelia figured that her parents were not from that same region of Quebec. Like her mother, Amelia and her sister were blonde. Meanwhile her father and brother had dark wiry hair. Her father's rough complexion hid his private thoughts. She knew there was much more to her family than the limited stories. Yet, like all other youth who were enthusiastic with all of the innovations and prospects offered in the 1960s, Amelia tended to think of the future rather than contemplate the past.

Unknown to Amelia and her siblings at the time, their grandfather—their father's father—lay buried in a makeshift graveyard near the Cree Community of Île de Fort George on

Hudson's Bay. Maybe Amelia's father concealed their Cree heritage on purpose. The appearance of his daughters clearly did not suggest such ancestry. Maybe he just did not want their lives to be compromised in any way.

The one aspect of her physique that was a benefit was her broad shoulders. Sports were a natural ability: pitching the baseball, hitting home runs, swinging a tennis racket. Balance, too, was an attribute for winter sports, especially skating. That the parish church had a massive acreage behind the hall provided access to field sports during the summer. The priests arranged for a rink to be flooded for hockey and pleasure-skating in winter. Long before it was ever considered an issue, these priests had already instituted a protocol that no cleric or adult could be alone with any young person. Volunteers were numerous, and the children's smiles more so.

Amelia's heart remained broader than her shoulders. So much of her spare time was devoted to others. She helped with the food baskets in the spring and winter. Parish calendars were delivered by her and several friends. Her acquaintances were many, and some were equally enthusiastic. It was a wonderful time to be young.

Her leadership was noted when she was still quite young. In the Brownies she assisted many of the girls in obtaining their badges. In the Girl Guides she was a patrol leader. The parish Junior Choir endeared her most of all. She had a vibrant range for Gregorian chant, Latin hymns, and Eucharistic Devotion. With her sister she sang at the early Mass on Sunday mornings.

The news shook the parish while Amelia was still in grade school. The parents of one of their classmates were killed in a motor vehicle accident. The responsible vehicle sped away remaining unidentified. At that time before the insurance industry offered Uninsured Motorist Coverage, the six children of the deceased were abruptly destitute. Amelia's family were one of so many offering to do whatever was necessary. Immediately those children had supportive care. Amelia attended to the emotional needs of her classmate, a young lady whose life had basically ended. Each day she'd be with her till nightfall. Amelia had no concept of fatigue.

As being the sole means to cope, talk of separating the children spread. Amelia was one of several young women who approached their parish priest stressing the need to keep the six children together. In turn, that idea was presented to the bishop. As a result, those six children did stay together. Volunteers helped with the maintenance of the family home. The parish absorbed the mortgage payments, while the diocese was ready to contribute if necessary. Women in the Catholic Women's League provided meals or attended every so often to prepare some. Amelia's mother was one of them. The children prospered academically, in social relationships, and later in life.

Then, as if that was not enough, during the summer following completion of grade school, another one of their classmates took ill. Dizzy spells were present but seemingly inconsequential at first. Months later the young lady died of a brain tumour.

In high school, Amelia's talents continued to open doors, or perhaps opportunities for others to employ her skills. The number of Catholic families unable to afford Separate School Education or choosing the public school nearby was ever increasing. To ensure continuing Catholic education for those children, the priests established Saturday morning religion classes from October to May. Amelia became one of the select few to teach religion to those children.

It bothered her greatly that, by her third year of high school, the number of families dependent on food baskets had doubled. Most new recipients were single parents. The increasing experience of divorce was rampant. Amelia loathed every suggestion that children of divorced parents didn't suffer. Society presented suggestions that sexual permissiveness prompted most separations. Amelia rejected that theory. Sexual relationships were not part of her social itinerary, and she vowed to never let them be so. She contemplated the religious life in her youth, and still considered same while avoiding the temptation.

In the final two years of high school, Amelia turned her attention from the Girl Guides to focus on charity work, particularly visiting the sick and infirm. She abhorred a reality in society that was all too prevalent. There were too many elderly citizens in those shelters simply because they were abandoned by their families. The irritating aspect was that the forsaken persons were generally those who had first financed the immigration of their families to Canada. Accordingly, that convalescent home received most of her visits. The grounds with a canopy of trees, winding path ways, decorative gardens, and flowing streams provided a spirited setting for the disillusioned. Because the complex was Catholic and operated by a religious order, the Stations of the Cross lined one pathway giving the residents and visitors the opportunity to share their faith. It was an inspiration, and Amelia gained much from the visits.

What should have been her last year of high school, under the direction of the Sisters of St Joseph, proved to be her hardest academically. Grade 13 demanded completion of departmental examinations. Although she was fluent in both English and French, and had acquired some verbal skills in Italian from visiting the elderly; Amelia's capacity at written examinations in English Literature, Grammar and Composition was lacking. As a consequence, in spite of all of her time generously spent for others, Amelia did not pass all of the required courses. She was successful in the second attempt which meant she graduated with her sister.

Distrust, dismay, and disenchantment raged throughout society during that last year of high school in 1968. The murders of Martin Luther King and Robert Kennedy, coupled with the anti-war riots, cities ablaze, and communist invasions in Europe, brought home that the world was no longer a peaceful place. Apollo 8 circled the moon on Christmas Eve while starvation spread across Africa. More had to be done, and Amelia suddenly started feeling very inadequate. All of the joys and enthusiasm of Centennial Year and Expo 67 were being quickly cut down to earth.

After high school, past friendships tend to become bleached memories of insignificant youth. With the start of university we parted. Amelia was no longer a part of that young man's life, the acquaintance to whom she could confess her worries with assurance of utmost privacy. The author was that young man who attests freely to her accomplishments, her generous soul, and her aspirations for a better life for all whom she ever met.

They taught each other how to look.into a person's soul and celebrate the goodness seen there. They did not date, nor did they ever exchange an overtly intimate moment. Amelia loved to talk, and the young man was keen to listen. If she had to stay late at the church rectory for receptionist duties, he would when called be there to walk her safely home. When the classmates got together for their annual bike trek, Amelia was always eager to ride; and he dutifully followed the group. A gentleman always did that, didn't he? Being the last in the line of bicyclists was assurance that others would not be hit by a following vehicle. It was these almost seemingly inconsequential acts that perhaps attracted Amelia to his style.

During their moments together, they remained abundantly clear that sexual contact was not anticipated. If they did embrace it was simply to share the warmth of each other's need. She taught him the importance of looking inside a person to observe that person's heart. Her laughter remained joyous, and her lively conversation was constant. They went in groups to the movies. She was so incredibly captivated by "The Sound of Music". Amelia even asked him to take her to see the movie again. Actually, she viewed it five times. When the young man mentioned that movie was close to his heart, she asked for an explanation. He offered that his father had found refuge in that convent after the war. He had been, along with so many others in the Polish II Corps, abandoned after the victory at Bologna.

"A Man for All Seasons" similarly captured her heart and soul. It was in her comments regarding defense of the papacy that he understood her commitment to the religious life. Amelia knew more about the reformation than most. She was most abrupt with her opposition to Protestantism in the sixteenth century that tried to eradicate the Corporal Works of Mercy. It had been the intention of Cromwell and Cranmer to decrease their importance with the argument that there was no need to strive for sanctifying grace when indulgences were anathema. "Can you imagine: what would they say if Martin Luther wrote the hymn, Amazing Grace?" At times her humour and quips could be cynical. However, to Amelia, her faith justified such expressions.

On one occasion someone mentioned the many who were tortured and even burned at the stake by both sides during the Reformation. Amelia was suddenly silenced. That was strange. She had often held that the end justifies the means, but at times dismissed that theory to accommodate a morally reasonable approach.

If there was ever an occasion that might have been considered a 'date', that occurred in the middle of August of 1968. High school graduation was two months in the past. He had been accepted at the University of Toronto starting September. Her noviciate would commence in November. After taking public transit, they boarded the ferry for the islands. There they spent the day talking aimlessly about everything. She was more direct than on other occasions. The elderly being abandoned, homeless children, loose morality, the growing drug culture, and the riots in Chicago the week before—all were given appropriate time to vent her frustrations.

After lunch at the dock restaurant, they continued their walk from Centre Island to Ward's Island. That route followed the path that brought them close to the beach. The young man recalled his earliest memories of the islands: the wooden walkway and the old stores where his parents had purchased his first plastic shovel and pail. Those buildings were no longer there. The memories received much description.

After passing by the small Anglican chapel they rested sharing the one beach towel he had brought from home. Amelia was unusually serious.

"I am Cree," she spoke matter-of-factly. He didn't understand, failing to hear her expression with the wind rustling the leaves in the poplar and maple trees. She repeated, "I'm Cree."

He thought he understood her words, but they didn't make sense. She was blonde with a fair complexion even in late summer. She mustn't have said "Cree."

Amelia continued with the explanation that her mother had heard from her family who still lived in a suburb of Montreal. Information was not complete but there was enough there to affirm what Amelia's parents already knew: that her father's father was Cree. She continued the tale, extrapolating freely to make sense of what she had previously heard. Together in those moments they were the most serious words they had ever shared.

"What does this mean?" His question tried to establish the consequences of the information.

She mumbled quietly, "I don't know."

He asked, hoping for her negative reply, "Will you leave?"

She had no answers to provide reassurance that the happy times would not suddenly disappear. Other children moved away with their parents. However this, she said, was different. Would she force herself to move because of who she discovered she was?

Her answer was not clear. For the entire day Amelia was humming one of Ian and Sylvia's recordings. The melody and lyrics of "Someday Soon" had always been one of her favourites. Then she turned to another song that echoed moments of uncertainty. The song "Changes" composed by Phil Ochs, eventually blossomed into lyrics that she sang quietly. By the time she reached the second verse, her words were clearly discernible.

> Moments of magic will glow in the night.
> All fears of the forest are gone.
> But when the morning breaks they're swept
> away by golden drops of the dawn of changes.
> Passions will part to a warm melody
> as fires will sometimes turn cold.
> Like petals in the wind we're puppets to the
> silver strings of souls of changes.
> Your tears will be trembling.
> Now we're somewhere else.
> One last cup of wine we will pour.
> I'll kiss you one more time, and leave you
> on the rolling river shore of changes.

That was her answer.

During the return trip onboard the ferry they shared their observation of the skyline. It was destined to change with the construction of several office towers. "Nothing remains." His words were sincere. He hugged her, holding her close in the evening breeze. They parted company that night with his kiss to her forehead. Friendship remained but as acquaintances they would go their separate ways.

Twenty years pass quickly when one is preoccupied with both trivial and serious activities, and is quite unable to discern the difference. The young man was older now. Friends in the neighbourhood and at university had disappeared into obscured horizons. Grey clouds covered most rainbows. Every aspect of employment proved stressful. Then, fortunately, office environs provided the opportunity to meet a young lady whom he delightfully married. That she was so much akin to Amelia in style and virtue created his Xanadu.

Years later, the concept for a reunion prompted enquiries to locate old friends. Only seven could be found, and each of those conveyed reluctance. Questions provided answers, some of which no one wanted to hear. Seeking a positive alternative, the young man prompted himself to enquire of the clergy at his old parish. There were some details about Amelia's family, and that information was freely shared.

Amelia did not remain in the convent. Her family returned to Montreal so that her mother could take care of Amelia's grandmother. Recessions had not been good for her father, and so he turned to self-employment. Amelia too returned to Montreal; and with that limited advice, information went silent.

Another seventeen years passed, and the world of social media allowed for more determined enquiries. More friends were located, and with them, information. Amelia's sister became a teacher and remained gainfully employed. As for Amelia, it was reported that she left Montreal and was working in social services distributing clothing to the needy. "The Corporal Works of Mercy in action," was the young man's immediate thought.

Within weeks, further information provided by clergy in Montreal confirmed she had truly returned home. Amelia was working with the Cree Nation providing clothes and nourishment. She had accomplished that which her soul had deemed to be most important. Her God was being satisfied with the aid she gave to those seeking her God. Those in the Cree Nation who Amelia touches with her kindness have reason to convey their appreciation.

3
EMILY

She sat in the restricted quarters, the stool wobbling beneath her frailty. Unable to escape the pressure of her occupation, the young girl buried her face in her palms. Long deep breaths failed to ease her sorry state. Her tears she could no longer hide.

The room was no more than a large cubby hole provided by her sponsor. After more than a year, she still didn't even know his full name. There were other terms describing his job, and more direct cat-calls describing her profession. She had done well. There was some applause. That really was the only reasonable expectation. Intelligence was not a factor. Having any esteem only got in the way. Flashing a broad smile and being able to enticingly ease flimsy attire from her thin frame were the only required skills. If there was an alternative, she would not be here. However, life affords few options; and God had never been kind to her.

In her fourteen years she had seen so much and shown more so as to attack the heart and soul of any principled individual. As the next girl entered the room, young Emily lifted her face from her palms to silently acknowledge the other stripper's presence. Nudity had become so commonplace in their lives, so much so that morality no longer intruded upon her dignity.

Peter Graves treated the summer student with some respect, as much as he could muster for anyone who was not his client. Confined to the stockroom on the second floor basement of the Ferguson Block, they worked together on a new government program: sending the appropriate Gross Weight Transport stickers to all of the provincial trucking firms. Graves would have preferred to be by himself. It wasn't just a matter of style. He had another agenda.

It was the third day of June, 1971, payday for the government employees. All paydays were good for Graves. He was going to be busy that lunch hour and then extremely occupied in the afternoon hours. That was the norm. Inner city standards were determined by their silent acceptance, not their validity, and clearly not by those established in the suburbs.

Peter Graves, still only twenty-three, had the respect of his co-workers and residents of his select community. He was acknowledged to always be the one to make generous donations to those in need. He carried himself confidently as if immune from any ill that could interfere with his plans.

There were no visible tattoos. Peter was always clean shaven and discussed any issue with a professional air. He was not tall nor heavy set. He had muscles mainly across his shoulders and upper chest. At about five-foot-six, he never drew anyone's immediate attention to his presence. However, to the influential in suburban society, he would not be welcome.

Graves belonged to the Hell's Angels. That was his true job. The government stockroom position with the Ministry of Transportation and Communications was his side-line. That position basically allowed him to earn a 'legitimate income' and file the appropriate tax return. He didn't have to do what the pimps, bikers, dealers and traffickers had to do to keep National Revenue at bay. Graves did not have to file a tax return for self employed income declaring his occupation as 'consultant'. He was basically nondescript except for the many that required and expected his services.

He never drove his bike to work except on the occasional Friday when he had to be on the shores of Lake Huron in the evening.

Among the so-called criminal elements of inner city society Peter Graves had incredible immunity. He had friends in Satan's Choice: an unheard of alliance, constantly involved in deadly turf wars. His friendships, though not open, provided access to information that kept Graves' hands clean and his territory secure.

Drugs were his game. On average, every payday, he pocketed over $16,000 from government employees alone. In today's currency that would be approximately $100,000. Working in the government, he was very much a fox in the henhouse. His customers were young and well-attired. The stockroom on the basement's lower floor was the hub of his operations. The stash was there, concealed in and behind boxes. He had enough $25 or $50 packages to satisfy all of his customers. There were a select few that required significant quantities so that they in turn could distribute the marijuana to their own clients.

Graves had his specific sources for the product. Lunchtime on Wednesdays he'd be at Union Station awaiting the CN Train and the delivery from Peterborough. The scenic venue of the Trent Canal provided the least suspicion. Similarly he had a supplier in the most prestigious area of Toronto—Post Road. Who would suspect anyone in the multi-million dollar mansions whose owners generously supported the politicians of the various governing parties?

Peter Graves kept his distance from the prostitutes and pornography. He had sufficient knowledge of these, enough to provide more than significant details of the intricacy of the operations. Other Hell's Angels members had been assigned those tasks to secure and patrol each of the locations. The entire program was complex, with the constant potential for sudden conflict. Locations had to be established, security had to be arranged, utilities had to be assured, pimps had to be organized, girls had to be obtained, customers had to feel secure, and people had to be trusted. The police also had to be assured that everything was within accepted standards, when in fact everything within the bikers' operation was a crime.

The Gay Community wanted their clubs and bath houses. That was an entirely new factor. Within weeks of the first demand, several establishments were open. Neither Hell's Angels nor Satan's Choice raised any territorial issues with respect to the Gay Community. That, for a while, kept the police at bay.

The increase in the number of girls from Quebec concerned him. Graves called it an "invasion." The entire network of strippers, hookers, pimps, truckers, and suppliers could cause inevitable bloodshed between the gangs. In Ontario, everything was reasonably docile. However, in Quebec, nothing was calm.

Even though it wasn't his prime interest, Graves was able to pinpoint the exact floor and wooden structure on St. Nicolas Street. The road was no more than a restricted laneway running south to north, parallel to Yonge Street to the east. At the southern end of St. Nicolas Street, the animal shelter was situated on Wellesley Street. St. Nicolas Street extended north to Bloor West, ending near various ritzy stores and cinemas. He shook his head after telling the summer student that the police knew of its operation, but nothing was being done to stop it. Street signs in the future reflected name changes first to Nicholas Street and then as the property increased in value to St. Nicholas Street. There was obvious intent to bury the past.

The author of this text is aware of Mr. Graves' involvement in all of these aspects of inner city life because he was the summer student assigned to complete the two month long task of preparing and mailing the Gross Weight Stickers to the many trucking firms. Allow us then to engage the first person singular in the rest of this story.

The conversations were not just about Graves. His questions were many concerning university life and courses, sports, and various novels. Based on the discussions, Peter struck me as being reasonably intelligent. More so, his connections were astounding. If you needed a wedding reception at an expensive hall, he knew the right person to ask. If you needed a certain product at half price, he'd get it for you.

Graves' reputation and activities were well-known to management in the department and to various government officials. Many concluded that the police had enough information to arrest him, but also surmised that he may have had value as a potential informant in the event of a major crime. Peter never directly mentioned any of his discussions with the police, but various comments suggested they had in fact taken place.

Many people feared Graves because of his trade. Everyone who dealt or trafficked in narcotics was considered a criminal.

Accordingly, these viewed Graves at a distance having heard remote rumors that in his youth Peter Graves had stuck a knife into the ribs of another teen causing him to fall from a subway platform. The incident involved an unpaid debt.

Be very assured that I wanted no part of Peter Graves and that project when I returned to the summer job in late May that year. The first year at the government was beneficial for income and financed the academic costs of university. Jobs were still limited, so there really was not much choice. Take what you can get.

Actually I had met Peter Graves in the first year at the government. He worked with others, and seemed so casual, and was always conversant and ready to laugh with people. Near the end of that summer there were rumours; I dismissed those, employing the theory that if they were real, then management would surely be doing something about it.

Management in the government offices at that time were usually occupied by war veterans. Upon returning from Europe the provincial government provided jobs within their departments. That decision was held in the highest regard, although the veterans in management preferred to avoid confrontation and just maintain peace within their ranks. Thus nothing was ever done even though the rumours were too numerous to avoid.

Graves considered me as diligent and supportive. Working quickly would get the job done. He was well onboard with that philosophy. Our productivity exceeded expectations in the first weeks.

It was during that first week that he opened a discussion by talking about the drug culture: not about him, but about Jim Morrison and Janis Joplin, mentioning their music, lyrics and deaths.

Whenever our discussion involved religion, his interest seemed sincere; however he quickly dismissed his need for it. The Pope was constantly doing something wrong, according to Graves. A longer conversation involved the homeless in the city. There were no conclusions, but the inference was clear that more had to be done. That issue was revisited particularly with respect to the city's decision to once again close Yonge Street between

King and Gerrard. There were several strip clubs along the less than two-mile stretch. The conclusion was quickly achieved that closing Yonge Street would benefit his businesses, generating more customers and profits.

As we approached lunch that Thursday, he politely invited me to eat with the others in our standard cafeteria. Graves remained behind to welcome his clientele.

Peter was always ready to express his gratitude. To show his appreciation, he handed me four tickets to a private party in a refurbished warehouse on Britannia Street off Dundas East. The women, flowing alcohol and access to weed were unrestricted. I found myself extremely uncomfortable. This was basically Club 54 in Toronto. Friends whom I had invited with the other tickets chose not to stay. I found myself stuck in the middle—working with a person whose lifestyle I considered undesirable.

The uneasiness I felt throughout that weekend certainly did not abate when we resumed work on Monday morning. Once again, Graves started talking about the thousands of street kids that had occupied the city's core. He attributed that, as did so many politicians, to the initial closing of Yonge Street the summer before. The entire area had become their protective haven. However, Graves avoided any admission that the closing of Yonge Street increased the profits of his establishments. The talk of the city core mysteriously prompted Peter to a discussion on territory. The Hell's Angels controlled the city below Dundas Street. North of Dundas including the Yorkdale area and several well-established high schools were the domain of Satan's Choice. The bikers never wore blazers, crests, or any attire to distinguish one from another. It was hard to suggest there was ever a difference in their methods or intended result.

I spent that lunch by myself, sitting in a bar that was not controlled by Graves or his bikers. The pork pie with a beer added to the refreshing break. Thoughts of just quitting the job performed a roller coaster ride through my brain. I so wanted to just get away from this, but financial constraints determined my answer. The funds were required for university. When thinking about salary and the cost of tuition, I pondered the reality that

these 'idiots' earning an annual government clerk's salary of about
$7,000 were in most cases being paid more than first year teach-
ers. Other thoughts continued the onslaught, ultimately demanding that I quit the summer job right that afternoon. I had to see
the manager.

He was not in, and Graves was waiting for me. His statement
was concise. "You're a good Christian person."

Shock and apprehension could not be separated.

"I need your help." He was almost begging. The explanation
had me even more astounded.

He had a problem with the clubs, particularly the number of
minors in the establishments. The request was simple: "We need
to get them out of there." Graves then stressed his compassion for
the homeless youth, albeit ironically. In the course of that almost
thirty minutes he mentioned Paul at the Zanzibar Tavern, Jersy
who worked at the racetrack, Paul Kent in Niagara, and empha-
sized the efforts at the Evergreen shelter, and Covenant House.

My reluctance continued to stump his impression. Questions
were many and he did not have all of the answers. By the end of
the day, nothing had been decided. We left accordingly with the
option to continue the conversation, if I so desired, the next
morning.

Rather than returning home, I stopped by the Zanzibar
Tavern, a well-known and regularly attended strip club. Paul was
there as Graves said he would be. Paul was an interesting fellow,
and not what one would expect in such a place. He stationed
himself near the door for security. Politely he always admitted
that the pimps were friends of the prior operator. These were the
ones who had been supplying women who were obviously
minors. Twenty-one was still the age for majority. After conjec-
turing that most teenagers appeared to look as if they were in
their twenties with the appropriate touch of make-up, Paul
advised they were concerned with the thirteen to sixteen-year-
olds. The situation possessed many dangers, primary of which
was the eventuality of angry pimps. Paul's reply provided some
assurance: "They'll not be a problem. Many don't want these
girls. If they just get rid of them, they could be charged with

abandonment." As we ended our discussion, I noticed a young brunette on stage fumbling her way through her routine.

The next morning was filled with questions conveying my interest and also various apprehensions. Graves reassured me with further information on the operations of each club, naming the respective persons, and even offering a bodyguard. My answer was in the affirmative once I heard security was in place.

Later that afternoon Peter handed me a list of fifteen names. Three were at the Filmores, five at Swayzee's near King Street, and seven at the Zanzibar. As such, Paul would only be involved in these last seven girls as he had no interest in the other establishments.

That night, Beach Boys' lyrics repeatedly echoed my expectations that were being tainted by fears of every possibility. "God Only Knows" captured some hope for success, but there was no assurance. As soon as there was momentary silence, dread instantly returned. Being always seemingly in control of circumstances had made life easy, almost too comfortable at times. Now I was being tested. "A good Christian? If Graves only knew." There were extremes to pinpoint any one virtue or vice. Reasonable expectations were all that were anticipated. "Just try," Graves had stated simply. But would the pimps who had the most to lose be so tolerable?

Manouane, an aboriginal community first settled a century before, provided no hope for any native resident. Agnielle had long experienced such despair. Thoughts of just ending her life had become her daily norm. The assembled cabins were a pathetic semblance of a village. The territory situated on the shore of Lake Métabeskéga was about five kilometers long with approximately two kilometers deep of cleared terrain. The nearest community was more than seventy kilometers away. Montreal was a distant dream to nearly every resident, more than two hundred kilometers to the southeast.

The population of about one thousand men, women and children in 1971 failed desperately to preserve traditions and the basic elements of their culture. Any chance of being assimilated into the white man's world was absolutely absurd. White men arrived, raped the land, and left. Logging was their primary interest. Taking advantage of the docile inhabitants seemed no less important. In spite of restrictions, the indigenous residents were still able to live off the land and fish the waters, but these activities were being crudely hampered by the commercial enterprises that provided little benefit for the reserve. There was definitely money being made but it all went elsewhere. In that respect, not much had changed in the sixty-five years since Atikamekw de Manawan was established as a reserve.

There was so much about the white men in their transport trucks on the gravel road that absolutely infuriated Agnielle. They abused the residents in ways so foreign to the passive nature of a proud self-sufficient tribe. They arrived in tidal waves. There was never just one but a flood of trucks transporting logs away from their precious lands. Acres were stripped bare and the river polluted, but there was no apology. Animals fled deeper into the woods making it almost impossible to secure game for meat or clothing. Every year they'd return just to repeat the destruction of land and water, to drive the animals farther into dense brush, and to pollute the air with fumes and noise. They drank till they could no longer stand, while prompting tribal men to join them. To appease any apprehensions there was enough booze provided to silence any objection.

Their chief fought the invasion as much as he could. The response of government had been lies, with the expectation that the native residents were so naive that they would believe everything Quebec City told them.

Agnielle's husband was fortunate to gain employment with a logging firm. It was while he was away from the community that Agnielle was raped. She conceived, telling her husband who arrived a month later that the child was premature and assuredly was his. However it proved impossible to convince him because the girl lacked his native appearance. Her husband left months later and she never saw him again.

Agnielle was thankful that the main attribute of the Manouane Nation was their insistence on caring for each other.

Her daughter Emily received as much support as possible from other families. The term 'cousin' meant so much, because the phrase truly affirmed that each person in the community belonged to the same family.

Quilting provided Agnielle with income. The finished goods were sent weekly to stores near or in Montreal. The truck drivers were at times willing to transport other items.

One tribesman had developed the expert skill to carve and whittle. Tree stumps and discarded logs became his canvasses. The intricacies of facial figures were astounding. Agnielle admired his work and the entrepreneurial skills necessary to get the most for the finished product.

Emily was seven years old when he moved into their household and shared their cabin. The young girl was happy. Her life had suddenly improved. After several truckers delivered sports equipment, she became active in various sports. Baseball and soccer were her best. School was her venue for attentive enthusiasm. Her mother was ever so at ease. Her vitality could easily be discerned. Because her mother was feeling so blessed, Emily was instinctively overjoyed.

It was a late summer evening when the whittler, unknown to two young girls, spied their evening swim in the lake. Emily was just eleven years old. Her friend was even younger. For whatever reason, when Emily returned to their cabin her mother was not there. While she was changing into her night clothes, the whittler had his way with her.

The girl could not tell anyone. She was too ashamed that she was violated. Emily knew that she wouldn't be believed and that the community might blame her for the incident. Unfortunately, he continued the attacks with threats demanding her silence. She was never accosted so as to fear pregnancy. Sodomy was his depravity. After having been raped on so many occasions, Emily, still only twelve years old, contemplated suicide. The thoughts were undeniably real. She had to escape the bleeding hell of such debauchery. One day a truck driver smiled at her in the local store. She sheepishly asked him for a ride. Emily knew what that would mean. She had heard enough stories of such trysts from the older girls. She took a chance and for favours granted, she found herself on the streets of Montreal.

The first visit to the Filmores proved that no one was to be trusted. There was no security. Nothing at all had been previously said to anyone there. Unfortunately that wasn't realized immediately. The girl called Blossom was an angry sixteen-year-old who wanted no part of any discussion. She declared she was there just to please her customers. Blossom was clearly well equipped for her profession, and accordingly chose not to conceal her attributes. She obviously did more than just dance. Two rough-looking characters watched from a distance. One was obviously her pimp, and the other possibly the club's manager. Her angry condescending tone continued to convey her frustration. She preferred discussions that generated sizeable bills on the table, but that was never my interest. The conclusion was simple, although she didn't have to specifically say it: she was not going to leave the premises. The response of her co-worker mimicked the first. There was to have been a third girl there, but she had left for another bar just two weeks before.

In the confines of the basement stockroom, Graves was challenged regarding the lack of protection. I was not about to surrender myself to thugs in some back alley. He offered no explanation, almost as if to say it was not my role to question him. His next line fell like a ton of bricks: "Oh yes, I should have said, 'The Choice operate that club.'"

Trust had nearly vanished. Such only complicated my role. Do I keep the pledge? The answer was simple. There really was no choice. I had basically become his 'Familiar', the devil's confidant or a sorcerer's pet in whom all faith and information had been entrusted. I had become Graves' pet pig. If I chose to bolt, I may not wake the next morning or even arrive home. The rumour about Graves knifing a debtor in front of a subway train was suddenly gaining more credibility. Graves was satisfied that I tried, and that there circulated among the clubs the opinion that having minors on premises was not and would not be tolerated.

Swayzee's Tavern provided successful results. The fact that there were so many rumours about the establishment closing prompted the girls and their sponsors to use any reasonable means offered to sever their relationship with the club. If they had just walked away, Hell's Angels would respond in haste. If a particular girl just left, even with the concurrence of her pimp, Hell's Angels would not be content. They were sure to pursue the flesh they owned. This then presented a menacing dilemma. I was acting for a member of Hell's Angels; however the bikers would never be wholly pleased with either result.

The young performers at Swayzee's were sixteen or seventeen years old. They clearly looked in their twenties. Surprisingly they were conversant. The pimps, having been informed, were agreeable. They had been promised a monetary compensation if any of the girls returned home. That agreement too presented a puzzle, as none of the girls had a home away from this profession. Four out of the five abandoned the trade, seeking shelter away from the industry. They were given opportunities for some retraining at George Brown College.

Efforts in two weeks produced satisfactory results. As we rested for the Dominion Day weekend, I was batting five hundred.

Before meeting any of the performers at the Zanzibar, I attended Greenwood Raceway to meet Jersy. As was promised, he kept court at the base of the stairway marked "A5". Spotting him from a distance, I wondered if I should laugh. He was the repulsive stereotype of a pimp. He was black with rough matted hair suggesting the grease had not been washed out. His bright pink floral shirt had a thin strip of fur inside the collar. The gold chain and broad gilded ring clearly suggested he had no knowledge of poverty. Then there was his tanned cane with the ivory handle.

All of my conclusions based on first impressions were so totally wrong. Jersy provided for homeless youths. Unlike the pimps who fed off the immorality of Yonge Street, Jersy kept teenagers away from the sexual dens. He treated lost teenagers as human: offering sympathy, help and understanding. Inheritance had given him access to a five-unit apartment that he converted into more rooms, enough for fifteen youths seeking basic shelter. Jersy had a network of assistants, firms and companies that could provide part-time or minimal employment. Unfortunately his work was limited to the east-end. He would not confront the bikers or any other element that could adversely affect the lives of those already in his care. It was not in my realm to grant him sainthood.

Jersy's very presence gave me hope. His information was even more reassuring. Like Graves he knew of Paul, the bouncer, and had heard rumours that many wanted "the babies" out of there. He never answered my query about the lack of police involvement. Out of the blue, totally unrelated to the flow of the conversation, Jersy asserted he was, "More concerned about the government doing nothing." He then went on at length about the porn shops, declaring his condemnation of the magazines that portrayed images of child pornography.

Before I returned to the Zanzibar, Graves had arranged for appropriate protection with additional bouncers at the rear. Success came quickly. Three girls who were less than sixteen years old begged to get away from the club and the industry. Contrary to his earlier advice, Jersy stepped in to provide temporary residence. Graves met the next day with the respective pimps to deliver the appropriate payments from his biker gang.

The fourth girl denied everything: particularly her age. She repeatedly swore she was in her twenties. Bitten finger nails suggested she might have just graduated from junior high school. She was more brazen than the others, trying to embarrass me by remaining topless. However, after more than a week of the same thing, it was candidly all too boring. She advised time and again that she had a place to stay, and didn't need my help. In this case, the pimp was all too willing to dump her. Paul had had enough of her. Apparently she did not get on well with the other girls. A lot of that temperament had to do with job titles. No girl ever called herself a 'stripper'. They were hired as a 'dancer'. If promoted they became an 'exotic dancer' or a 'feature dancer'. It was at that time that I realized there was more to that profession than just wanting to stay or leave. This girl, who dismissed her nudity, thought more of what she had to do to get that next promotion.

After the week ending July the 9TH, I rested several days before considering the final three. Seven girls were able to leave the claws of depravity. The fate of the other five remained in their own hands.

The next two grabbed the offers to escape street life. By that time I was relying on Covenant House for assistance in providing shelter. Jersy had reached his limit. Government assistance seemed limited to hostels and food banks such as the Victor Mission and St. Vincent de Paul Society that were designated to help only the older men. However, many churches were becoming an inspiration to those less fortunate. The parable of the Good Samaritan was bringing to life some assistance in such a monumental task.

Graves was pleased: nine out of the fourteen were no longer a problem. Out of the five that he considered "an impact," three were not his problem, and one was working for a club that would soon be closed.

I recognized the girl right away, not because of her naked features, but from her short stature and her uneasiness. Like the others, Emily tried to impress me with her nudity. I took off my shirt and told her to cover herself. The fact that she did it right away told me that she was not yet sixteen.

She concealed information as if it was to her benefit not to be honest. That was a common trait in that profession. Honesty like all other virtues only got in the way. When I asked about her parents, she evaded any response. Then when I asked about her mother, she fought to withhold the tears. Conclusions are achieved quickly in that profession. I surmised she was either raped or abused by a family member. Realizing her frailty, I pledged to return the next day. In a child's voice she whispered, "Thank you."

Before meeting with her on July 21ST, a brief discussion with her protector was compelling. Stressing the reality that the girl didn't even know his name, and that she had been "seized from

Quebec" allowed me to suggest the obvious conclusion that she had been kidnapped. A terse lesson on the Napoleonic Code assured him he had no defense. Thereafter, he pushed the idea that Emily was no longer welcome at the Zanzibar. Clearly he was not about to admit fault for keeping her there.

The meeting with her on the 21ST was eventful. Details flowed from her heart. Her candid tone was that of an adult even though she was still two weeks shy of her fifteenth birthday. She fled the native reserve but avoided talking about the exact reason. Emily didn't know if her mother was still alive. She provided a vivid description of the impoverished state of her aboriginal community, suggesting the issue of sustenance caused her flight. In the latter course of that conversation her enthusiasm ebbed, having been replaced by a distraught expression. Anything would do as an alternative to her present situation. Her commitment was complete. Emily quietly bid farewell to the other girls that evening.

The next morning, I skipped work to meet Emily and take her to the train station. She assured me that she would be okay. That I doubted, and accordingly notified the appropriate railway staff to safeguard a minor during her trip. The Department of Indian Affairs had also been contacted to await her arrival in Montreal.

Emily was more apprehensive than I expected when we shared breakfast that morning. She smiled, but her tone was distinctively cautious. Just as we were about to leave the restaurant and cross the street to the train station, she dropped her bombshell.

"I am not going home." Her statement had me aghast. "He won't shove it up my ass again." Emily couldn't have been more direct. She admitted that she had in fact been raped and sodomized. Her sobs were endless. Tears flowed, dropping from her cheeks onto the napkin. "Please?" she begged.

I couldn't blame her in the least. Trying to console her was difficult standing on Front Street across from Union Station. My mind demanded reason. What now? Emily was still counting on me.

Her tears did not respond to any attempt at compassion. "I'm sorry," was not sufficient.

I continued stating that I understood and would do whatever was possible to accommodate her needs. At the same time I privately cursed our Prime Minister and his statement four years prior that had been often repeated on the nightly news: "The Government has no business in the bedrooms of the nation." Looking at Emily with as much sympathy that I could feel, I personally condemned Pierre Trudeau and vowed to never vote Liberal again. The government had to be involved to stop such sexual activities and to prevent children such as Emily from being attacked.

Emily did not take the morning train. A telephone call to Montreal notified them not to expect anyone at the train station there. The counter clerk was also alerted to not provide supervision on the train. Meanwhile the ticket was changed for passage on the mid-day train.

We talked for the next hour, both of us searching for any sense in life. Emily finally started considering alternatives even though they may have been just wild dreams. Having been paid the day before, I handed her my weekly salary. She had my telephone number and address. I pledged to do whatever I could to help her. She gave me a hug and then boarded the train; it was the last time I saw her or heard from her.

"Ten!" Graves was surprised. He was never told that a report to the government and police was being planned. I personally couldn't count on the Hell's Angels or any biker gang or conglomerate of pimps to do what was best for such young innocent people. Every child is entitled to a childhood.

Before the end of the summer, Graves' ugly character controlled several conversations. He vowed that one day he would die in a shootout with the police. His activities in the drug culture were becoming too insecure. He had stupidly spoken too often to too many people whom he thought were his friends. By the end of that summer he could trust no one. I returned to university in September and never met Graves again after Labour Day.

Years later, the news stunned me, but I shouldn't have been surprised. Peter Graves did die, having been shot in an exchange with the police. An alias was used so the death record never conveyed his name. A poor-man's burial was his farewell to this earth.

The age of majority was reduced to eighteen. Those who would have been considered 'minors' suddenly became legal. As the city continued with the pedestrian mall each summer, more and more young teens flooded into desperate situations. A shoeshine boy was found murdered six years after Emily left the city. The depravity had not changed.

The man named Kent, whom Graves had described as "Our man in Niagara", died after his vehicle left the roadway and somersaulted into a field. The brake line was cut.

Paul at the Zanzibar passed away in 2003 after many years of extending care to those who sought his protection. Pimps and dancers came and went, but his commitment to assist the young never died.

Jersy was not present at Greenwood Raceway throughout its Centennial Celebrations in 1975. Enquiries affirmed no one recalled him. His silent virtue and discreet acts of kindness will only be remembered by those he helped.

I never met nor spoke with Agnielle. Reports on First Nation communities confirmed the abysmal conditions. Children would go missing, and women would mysteriously disappear. Regarding those who may have been found, chances are they were not alive. Each had a tale. Each had a family. Each had dreams that were never fulfilled.

I never heard about Emily again. My one letter received no response. Did she return to the native community? Did she stay in Montreal, or move elsewhere in the province? What was she doing? Was she even alive, or did she suffer a horrible death? Where was she?

Prayers are still said for the many young women such as Emily who lose their innocence to predators, who wander the streets, or are held captive in the vulgarities of hellish depravity. It is never forgotten that the last day I saw her, spoke to her, and gave her hope and a hug was the Feast Day of St. Mary Magdalene.

4

BRENT

Hold on to what is good
even if it's only a handful of earth.
Hold onto what you believe,
even if it's just a tree standing by itself.
Hold onto what you must do,
even if it's far from here.
Hold onto your life,
even if it's easier to let go.
Hold onto my hand,
even if I'm away from you.

The insurance clerk paused, having read this Pueblo Prayer to himself. It was his daily mid-morning ritual being drawn to the simplicity of the verse amid the tensions created by unrealistic managerial expectations. After glancing out the third floor window, he meticulously placed the laminated prayer card inside his jacket pocket and continued with the next file.

The pile of new correspondence had been unusually light that week considering the staff vacation schedule that compelled remaining workers to double their tasks. Customers' needs still had to be addressed. There was the inevitable reality that more time would always be spent answering telephone complaints if correspondence wasn't answered promptly. Brent accordingly devoted the time necessary to keeping the customers satisfied.

People were experiencing a strange angst that summer of 1973. Inflation was starting to escalate prices while wages remained stagnant. There was an incredible hike in the price of fuel, a situation created by a previously inconsequential group called OPEC. In the Middle East, hatred had sparked another war. Strikes were rampant in Britain, with similar activity threatening this side of the Atlantic. South of the border, the United States was ready to impeach its President. The war in Vietnam was no closer to resolution as pictures of body bags and coffins continued to occupy the evening news. Seven years had passed since Expo 67 and that enthusiasm was near dead. Canada had just barely beaten the Soviet Union in hockey nine months before. That spirit of dominance would last just another year. In New York, a horse called 'Secretariat' accomplished what no other steed had done in twenty-five years. There was much to raise one's enthusiasm, yet more to generate concerns.

Nationally, Prime Minister Trudeau and his minority government were continuously engaged in aggressive negotiations with the steadfast Progressive Conservatives. Abortion was legalized in an 'omnibus bill'. For the aboriginal communities, not much was being accomplished or even planned. The interest of the government focussed on controlling prices and inflation, rather than improving the lot of the average Canadian.

Everyone has an opinion on perceived government inefficiencies. Brent had his views, very solid opinions of what should and could be done. He struggled to appreciate any of the Liberal Government's efforts to help those who required assistance the most. Native Canadians were basically abandoned with the selection of the particular Minister of Indian Affairs. Jean Chrétien, even though he would more than two decades later become Prime Minister, appeared, in the eyes of many in the aboriginal community, to be just babysitting a time bomb. Brent loathed the man as much as he deplored the repulsive title. Native Canadians were not just an 'Affair'.

Brent never brought his tribal card to work, or carried it in his wallet. Just knowing it was available if ever needed was important. Brent was of Mohawk descent, born in 1947 into the ancestral community bordering the eastern coast of Lake Simcoe. About his parents, he was forever admiring their lifestyle and decisions. They understood the inherent peril of being recognized as "Indian" in a white man's world. His parents didn't need long detailed lectures to realize the consequences of that particular abhorrent phrase in the British North America Act that segregated members of the native community into the same restrictive group with the insane. They willingly took the chance that life away from the reserve would be better while remaining true to meaningful principles respecting nature and humanity.

Their house had no basement. It was basically a wooden structure built upon an elevated block foundation. Even in his earliest years, he knew he was fortunate. The lot was incredibly large. He could run for minutes to get to a line of trees, and then be able to scamper through the brush to the stream bordering the farthest extremity of someone's property. There were no fences, just freedom to explore. They had a well. Purification techniques had been supplied. Hydro was available. Heating was an oil furnace with regular fuel delivery. An antenna assured reception of five channels on their black and white television. The fridge was small, but functional for the three occupants of the two-bedroom house.

Off the reserve, in a rural setting occupied predominantly by non-tribal residents, his parents inevitably experienced the double standards of society in the early 1970s. Tribal card holders were paid less, if they could ever find employment. That wasn't a sudden occurrence. It had always been the case. Brent's father commenced attempts to overcome that obstacle by investing in hair colour. Grooming was more essential than ever to assure the desired appearance. A lighter shade of brown hair did the trick. Acquired plumbing skills from the reserve generated employment. Brent's mother too was able to land a clerical position after disguising her appearance. In his heart, the child cursed that reality: that a person had to become who he or she wasn't in order to just put food on the table. Regardless of what he may have thought in his youth, once he was in his teens Brent also abandoned his native appearance to promote possibilities of personal success. He had no plan to return to any reserve permanently. He already had learned so much from his parents: about the beauty of nature with all of the myths and lore of the indigenous communities.

After completing grade eleven, during the summer of 1964 he naively left the family home expecting immediate employment in Toronto. All he found was temporary accommodation at a hostel. Brent was too presumptuous to realize he was lucky. It took only a day for him to despise so much about everything in the big city. There was no comfort, no compassion, and very little hope. Fortunately, a woman, doing charity work on behalf of an organization called Covenant House, offered a glimmer. Initially her assistance was no more than better clothing. At least he had an umbrella and pants that were not in shreds.

Her devotion to his cause became more than just clothing. He had been called a 'vagrant', but the woman never used that term. Brent actually preferred the term 'vagrant' compared to the prospect that someone might call him 'Indian'. He never specifically mentioned his parents although he had to reveal his prior residence. Using "Beaverton" for the name of the town obscured many realities.

Brent clearly understood there were others whom she was also assisting. With that thought, he was suddenly sensing competition. The teen wanted the jobs the woman might offer other vagrants. He wanted to be the one to be employed. Patience was not his virtue. It didn't exist. Brent had to overcome that coarse disposition but had difficulties as he didn't even know it was an issue. It took the woman's stern lecture to finally convince him. Later in life he was thankful that he chose to listen. Suddenly his impetus changed, generating opportunities.

He amazed himself with his ability to learn skills. The first job did not pay much, but it was clerical. Fortunately there was a strange unexplained reality at the time: workers were leaving jobs to be employed elsewhere. That gave Brent and all others in similar positions opportunities to advance. He was not going to be hampered.

During employment, no one knew about his native heritage. He kept that a secret, and worked the silence to his benefit. At one point he had to provide a copy of his birth certificate. When it finally arrived, there was no mention of his parents' native status. That happened quite often, he was later told: almost an act of kindness by the maternity ward.

His parents remained an active part of his life, until his mother's death. His father remarried less than a year later and moved on, leaving Brent by himself. Work soothed his solace, and fortunately provided a further opportunity for promotion. He learned fast, taking the necessary courses. The office on Bay Street had become his second home. Brent appreciated the opportunities the insurance realm gave him to help others. He was loath to mention this appetite to his co-workers as many had already considered him somewhat strange. Nonetheless, Brent was always able to smile at the end of the day.

As he read the adjuster's report with all of the specifics of vehicle damage and investigation, Brent quietly hummed his usual litany of tunes from the movie 'Oklahoma'. The independent adjuster's report was formatted in the usual style: identity, policy particulars, police report, cause and damages. Reports had become rather repetitious with the style being copied in each letter. Ultimately everyone claimed innocence and more damages than had actually occurred. Honesty was no longer a factor. The only variable in the perception of honesty was the truth; and it was his role to determine reality. In that respect he was no different from any other adjuster, being the investigator and judge on every decision. It was not easy for Brent because he really wanted to please everyone. Unfortunately, insured persons, the claimants and his employer did not all share the same interest. Claims handlers were always being told they were paying more than they should. Having to report to the shareholders in some foreign land was the duty of management.

"Surrey with the Fringe on Top" was interrupted by Dorothy's telephone call. This was not his favourite client, as she pestered him at least every second day regarding his liability investigation even though the woman clearly ran a red light.

The rest of the afternoon started to drag with the daily queries concerning the whereabouts of their department manager.

Ross was clearly a decrepit middle-aged individual who had the morals of a tom cat, and the drinking capacity of a fish. The truth, as ugly as it was, confirmed the rumours that Ross was personally delivering new claim reports to an independent adjusting firm so it could earn fees in exchange for booze, stag films and hookers—at least twice per week. Senior management knew about the fiasco as, on several occasions, Ross in his drunken state had been sent home early. After a while even the office manager in his polluted condition knew enough not to return to the office before five o'clock. That way he wouldn't be seen and would avoid being chastised. Two years later Ross died in an accident. He had stumbled into a car for a ride home with a drunk driver. The front page of the newspaper the next morning pictured Ross partially hanging outside the passenger window with the vehicle still wrapped around a light standard. That was the bleaker side of the insurance industry, in particular that office. Not everyone was one hundred percent committed to their job and public service. However, Brent was.

Before leaving the office that night, he packed the necessary papers in his satchel. Among these, there was a proof of loss form. The burglary had been astonishingly quick, suggesting to the police that the culprit had known the total layout of the residence. The homeowners were aware of this and suspected their long lost son. Accordingly, they wanted the entire issue resolved hastily. The police had their suspicions and the family had their interests. Whether they would even continue with the claim was also questionable.

Brent was most diligent in his discussion with the family. After more than an hour discussing alternatives and figures, the proof of loss was signed for a figure far less than the amount stolen. They recorded the cause as 'mysterious disappearance'. That way the police would discontinue their enquiries, and any suspicion of their son would be dropped. They smiled as Brent concluded the meeting with the assurance to have the funds issued the next day.

He had looked at the elderly couple throughout the meeting, admiring their obvious love for one another. "How beautiful!"

Brent always cherished such scenes of familial intimacy where smiles conveyed such happiness together. At the same time he regretted that he would never personally experience such wonder. It wasn't that he had given up on that prospect. He had loved and had lost. Once was enough. Actually, Brent had never married. He and the young lady chose to live common-law. Having met her seven years prior, he always felt it would last forever.

Ariane was her name. From the first instant, they seemed so totally committed to one another. Even their heritage, though not from the same clan or tribe, drew them together. In fact, that awareness created an effervescent energy as they were both clearly committed to their ancestors and to their lives together in all aspects of the world's allurement.

Ariane's name alone established a mystical aspect to their relationship. Brent loved the study of the antiquities, especially Greek mythology. He recognized that her name was derived from Ariadne who was the daughter of King Minos and thus the grand-daughter of Zeus. Ariadne was in charge of the labyrinths that were designed to protect those to be sacrificed to Zeus. However she decided to free the captives, thus creating conflict between the deities and humans. In similar fashion, Ariane was a most merciful person, always keenly interested in the tribulations of the impoverished while wishing to do as much as possible with the little they could afford.

Her wide brown eyes clearly displayed her various emotions. They were so demonstrably expressive. Her smiles, her grins and troubled expressions were also easy to discern. Her tawny complexion appeared to embrace a heart overflowing with desire. Nothing could be concealed. There was no hurdle she did not try to jump or mountain she could not climb. Her long black naturally-matted hair was more often than not curled with various beads. Feathers she never wore as she questioned the idea of depriving any bird or water fowl of the means for its natural warmth. Ariane was very much a vegetarian, reserving meat for only one meal per week. As a cook she surpassed expectations.

Ariane rarely left the house without Brent. He drove the car; she did not. He carried the groceries, opened doors and maintained the yard. Brent did everything a gentleman was supposed to do, and appropriately she let him. She wanted to be dependent upon him.

Brent had met Ariane during his first trip to Montreal. Expo 67 beckoned them as it did so many millions. Together with three young men from the Rama Reserve, with whom he had stayed in touch, they completed the trek in a 1964 Cougar Convertible. The vehicle belonged to the father of one of the passengers. Brent happened to be the only one with a license, so he became the designated driver. During the trip, the son, whose father owned the car, mentioned Kahnawake. The suggestion was made because of his acquaintance with members of the community, and as they needed an inexpensive place to stay.

It was about two hours before midnight when they arrived. Accordingly the greeting was polite among aboriginal persons. Two of the vehicle's passengers were offered rooms in an old log house. Sleep was not the best. The next morning, Brent met Ariane. By midday they were to have been at the Expo site. Brent delayed leaving as long as possible, just to be around the young lady even though her chores confined her to the smoke house.

The connection was made, and both young persons were aroused. Two weeks later, Brent returned to Montreal by train. It was wonderful being young.

By the time 'Man and His World' continued Expo's legacy in the summer of 1968, Ariane and Brent were living together in Toronto. From the start she felt rather uncomfortable within the big city. At least being outside Montreal gave her some independence and allowed her to be part of the rural community—their natural environs. Conversations shared prospects for their future. However, regardless of their dreams, there always remained the impact of their present lifestyle on their ability to maintain their heritage. Brent willingly talked of his parents, especially his father's prowess and success. He did so to convince Ariane that there was a benefit to partly forsaking the past. But in doing so, he ultimately had to admit that he did not know of his father's whereabouts. That bothered Brent more and more with time.

Ariane's story was remarkably different. She advised that her parents could trace ancestors on her mother's side to Arizona and the Shoshone tribe. At times, she wasn't so sure and used to also mention Hopi and Pueblo. There was vagueness as to exactly when and why her mother came to Quebec. The more that Ariane spoke about it, the more evident it became that it was against her will. There remained within the young woman the inkling to return to the southwest and more fully explore her heritage. The description in books of the western United States was too generic. Television westerns had done her ancestors injustice.

Socially, Brent and Ariane were not active. Whereas he had successfully disguised his native appearance, she chose to remain 'faithful' to her culture. She never verbally questioned him about such matters, but in her heart she knew who she was, and was not willing to obscure that. Beads continued to adorn her dark hair. Her attire displayed her dark tanned arms, shoulders and legs. Sandals were the norm. She never once wore high heels. Accordingly, office summer picnics and Christmas socials were not on the agenda. Religion was a questionable item with more faith being attributed to her lore and customs. Attendance at any church was not a ritual.

It was in September of 1973 that Brent was suddenly consumed with the necessity to talk with someone. Events in late 1972 had taken their toll. For almost a year they lay buried. He continued with work diligently while his dreams were obscured by a sudden sand storm.

Ariane ventured to Arizona after Labour Day that year. With Brent's concurrence she was to affirm her heritage and experience the southwest native traditions. Prior to her departure, she had talked about her "El Pueblo Llano", her 'common people'. She was clearly searching for that missing ingredient in her past and Brent cherished her inquisitiveness. Ariane telephoned several times after her arrival, and then the phone went silent. She never returned. Brent held out hope considering all that they had

shared together. They both belonged to the expansive influence
of the Mohawk culture. That had given them both a heritage to
share. Although he never reckoned it, she wanted more than just
the past. Ariane wanted the present. She wanted to live the aboriginal life. Brent, however, remained pragmatic. He knew all
too well he could not totally embrace the native lifestyle while
expecting to provide for his spouse away from the reserve.
Returning to the restrictions of Indian culture for him would
never happen.

The author of this text was the fortunate one to be entrusted
with the account of Brent's life. He worked in Brent's office.
Their desks, long before the age of cubicles, were distant from
each other. The author was one of only a select few to never
question Brent's lifestyle. Some of the office chatter even spread
rumours that his girlfriend left because Brent was 'gay'. How they
ever knew she left, Brent could only guess. The comments hurt,
deeply at times, affecting his emotional stability. Yet, he was man
enough to dispel their adversarial impact when it came time to
helping the public. Whatever the rumours or innuendoes may
have suggested, Brent held firm to the hope that Ariane would
return. However, time is not always the optimist's friend.

Our first meeting took place on a Friday night after work.
Brent's revelations caused considerable dismay, a reaction that
coloured further information during subsequent discussions.

Brent remained passive, and at times out of character for several months after our initial conversation. Charity and friendship
ultimately provided opportunities to talk some more when the
occasion seemed right. In the summer of 1974, Brent applied for
an internal promotion. The door closed quickly, favouring
another employee whose work-ethic was far less than acceptable.
Brent and so many in the office and in fact in the entire industry
knew that it was not an issue of how well you did, but who you
knew.

Once the door closed, Brent realized his time with the company was at an end. Before Thanksgiving of 1974, he was gone.
Someone suggested he was working for an insurance company
near Barrie. Another co-worker suggested the destination was

east toward Ottawa. Brent was not heard from after he left the office. The legacy of a particular Native Canadian excelling with an insurance company on Bay Street was never recorded. The sad reality, according to his own conclusion, was that if management had ever known of his ancestral background, he would never have been hired, let alone given the chance to advance.

More than three decades later, Brent's seven-line obituary appeared in the newspaper.

5

KAREN

The brutality of her rape stunned the listener. Suddenly the vibrant soul had become a pathetic quivering wretch. Incoherent phrases recounted the loss of her innocence. Enraged expressions continued, declaring the totality of her violation, a devastating act that more than a decade later could without warning cause her emotions to suddenly erupt.

Her supervisor always scheduled employee interviews after normal work hours. By 5:10PM the office was routinely empty. This generally provided adequate time without interruptions to discuss performance and set personal objectives.

Karen was a devoted employee. Her customer service was incredible. In the public evaluation forms no one ever complained of her performance. She was well on her way to completing her associateship courses that were routinely recommended for all staff. However, in her case, she was clearly exceeding expectations: completing the required curriculum faster than anticipated. Karen had many friends within the office, making her a valuable asset with respect to teamwork.

Not much was ever known about any employee's personal life. Vague questions concerning such were no longer allowed during the initial interview or at any time thereafter. Staff got to meet spouses or friends at Christmas parties. Some workers might have mentioned their families or vacations. However, between a supervisor and the worker, personal matters were a forbidden realm.

Karen was a slight individual, maybe five foot two inches. Her pale complexion suggested she had an aversion to sun light.

She was frail suggesting a vegetarian diet. Her dark hair was short, and cleanly scented. She took care of herself to the same extent she took care of her clients.

Describing Karen's activities as a team player was a simple task. She participated in every company event, and attended every staff gathering or party. Laughter was so common: not at people but with them. She knew how to converse freely and at times controlled endless conversations. Two drinks at any gathering were her limit. She made everyone certain of that. There were many such social events. Several employees opened their houses to such festivities: summer barbecues, Thanksgiving, Valentine's Day or birthdays. Accordingly, the department received many accolades regarding how well everyone worked together.

Other events within the department were not going so well. The supervisor had to deal with a reality that his own boss—the regional manager—was absolutely disliked. There were issues of insufficient wages and minimal salary increases. His style gave no confidence to any promise. Affecting that whole scenario were two major issues. Most insurance companies were not awarding significant salary increases to existing staff. If a worker wanted more than two percent increase, he or she had to join another company. Then there was the world wide inflation crisis with universal rates ranging between 14% and 22%. Young workers had loans and credit cards forcing them into the world of persistent collection agencies. It was not a good time for any employee. Thus a heavier onus fell upon a supervisor to be most assuring in a tone that calmed tensions and encouraged hope.

Those were the variables to be considered on that late afternoon in February, 1981. The office was small with lightly coloured walls and an opaque-glass door. The supervisor was ready to praise the employee, assure her of an immediate 1.5% increase in salary with an accompanying pledge for a further increase on her anniversary date. He did however have two other comments to make. These were essential as no employee could ever be made to feel they were achieving one hundred percent efficiency.

In the month prior, Karen had settled a total loss claim on an older vehicle when the broker was adamant that the insured person had arranged for the vehicle to be torched. The insurance broker did not want his loss record at all affected by such criminal matters. He had already assured himself that the circumstances affirmed his decision. That insured person had previously lived on the regional native reserve, and the torched remains were found in a field about one mile from the insured person's residence. That older vehicles were being reported as stolen and found torched on the reserve was not an uncommon occurrence. In that particular case, the police had limited investigation as the torched vehicle gave no clue as to who had driven it there or why it was set on fire. However, there always remained the common query, "Who has the most to gain?"

Karen had taken a meticulous approach in handling that file. After her own research and realizing the police investigation could not support a denial, she arranged for the settlement. The amount was well within her settlement authority.

The supervisor's second issue involved another claim: the theft of stock. The merchant's expertise was 'Canadiana'. His stock was predominantly Arctic prints and Inuit carvings. There were few people at the time who valued such commodities. Most of this vendor's stock had been sold to visitors and tourists particularly American. The evaluation of replacement cost was thus a perplexing issue. With respect to the crime, the Police had no leads. The front door was clearly damaged. There was no requirement for an alarm. Prior sales were significant, and the merchant had no reason to believe that they would not continue.

Karen arranged a settlement at 72% of the merchant's declared replacement cost value. The stolen items themselves were not replaced yet as the vendor planned to attend Frobisher Bay later that year and at one time purchase an extensive stock to last another year. Opinions in the office suggested the payment should have been no more than fifty percent until he actually replaced the goods.

In spite of the employee's fundamental decisions, and that the supervisor generally did not disagree, the issues had to be mentioned if only to affirm the reality that no employee is perfect.

Her exclamation was brief and concise, but it was not the end. Should her supervisor have expected any other response? The place of her birth was unknown to him. Her early life had clearly not been his interest. Even that she was born and raised in Thompson, Manitoba was unknown to him. The application for employment always remained within her personnel file to which a supervisor never had access. All he knew of Karen's past was her employment for a couple of years with Manitoba Public Insurance.

That provincial government insurance plan began in 1971, being the pledge of the New Democratic Party to control the cost of claims. Insurance claims were inevitable, and elsewhere the costs were escalating beyond all reasonable expectation. Labour rates for auto repairs in Ontario had increased more than six hundred percent in ten years, while Manitoba was able to control that labour rate as well as the cost of treatment and medication for injured persons. There was much to be said for the insurance plan that many called a 'scheme', but it was effectual in its ultimate design. Accordingly, insurance employees in Manitoba were well-trained, had the assurance of employment and union benefits, and had reasonable expectations for their future. As to why Karen left Manitoba, her supervisor never asked.

Karen continued with her response, clearly suggesting the interview would not be quick.

"They're tired . . . tired of being falsely accused."

Her supervisor candidly could not disagree with her conclusion in the case of the torched vehicle as the police investigation had nothing to offer conclusively regarding the culprit.

"I understand them." Karen considered it necessary to repeat the obvious.

The supervisor was about to mention that they always had to consider the 'motive' and who had the most to gain.

Before he could say another word, she continued, "I saw it all. This is nothing new." She then controlled the conversation with dramatic commentary of several claims she handled in Manitoba.

The first she accomplished using the shock factor. This also involved a torched vehicle. However, in that case, there was a child still in the rear seat. "Do you know what it's like to see pictures of the remains of a dead child covered in lye? Just to control the smell? Tell me, do you?"

He was silent.

Karen's description continued focussing on her Manitoba supervisor's disdainful opinions. "He told me to tell the family that it was our decision that the child's father set the car on fire. Bullshit! Could you believe anyone would have ever done that? There isn't a man alive that would do such a thing!"

The present supervisor's shocked expression was firm.

"There was no police report. No gas can. No motive. The father was not well off, but he was employed. Why would he kill his daughter? Even the police had no interest in the investigation." Karen identified the police force as the RCMP.

Her disgust with false accusations seemed clearly understood. To make sure there was no misunderstanding, Karen continued. She chose to justify every decision she had ever made.

Regarding the merchant's stolen goods, she was adamant telling her supervisor that there was no motive for that vendor to have arranged for the theft of his stock noting he had to replace the stock to continue his business. "However," she added, "it was never going to be the same quality."

His slightly puzzled expression conveyed his need for more.

"You know ivory is scarce. There's no more to be had. A carving with any ivory is definitely more valuable than one with plastic replicas. Second quality never sells as well."

He couldn't disagree.

"I went there to his store, at lunch time, about two weeks before he settled. To carry away that much stock of Inuit carvings, whoever it was would have needed a truck. There was construction with many workers in the area at the time. The boxes he had in his store would not have been strong enough to cart away those goods. Someone, whoever took them, had to have their own containers. There's no evidence that he ever had such containers in the back room."

The supervisor was satisfied with the response, and ready to move on. The office cleaning staff had arrived. Regardless of there being an ongoing meeting, they had no trouble running the vacuum cleaners at full thrust.

"Ya, okay, about paying close to replacement without receipts, he needs the cash on hand to buy the replacement stock. He couldn't do that with the amount that others have suggested." Karen then extrapolated on the wholesalers and marketing venues for Eskimo carvings near Thompson. Clearly she was very erudite on the issue. She obviously deeply embraced that entire region, or so he thought.

Ultimately her comment that she was happy to leave changed the entire tone of their conversation. To that point she had very much held the upper hand with him being attentive to her description and comments supporting her decisions. This was a compassionate and understanding person whose heart was more expansive than the frailty of her physique.

With the change in tone, Karen suddenly became hushed. It was a worrisome silence. The cleaners had completed their chores in that portion of the office. Their vacuum cleaners were mute. Karen's silence started to resound.

Suddenly the tears appeared. He was stunned. Quickly they flooded her cheeks. She shivered, clasping her palms to her face. His comments followed, but they were inconsequential. He felt most feeble. Karen continued in her morose state, her face dipping forward to the boardroom table. Reacting, he stepped outside the office for a box of tissues. He never brought the tissues to any meeting as he always figured their absence would not encourage tears of anger or frustration. This time, he was clearly not prepared.

The office clock chimed seven times before she said a word. Karen stared straight ahead and then slowly shook her head from side to side.

"He raped me." She could barely offer the words. Then her silence caused him to be even more concerned. "He raped me," she continued.

The supervisor immediately thought it was an office issue.

"I told my mother, but no one believed me."

Her tale with every uncomfortable expression consumed nearly half of a box of tissues. Her tears remained incessant. Her voice shook, barely audible at times.

Karen was ten years old at the time, being twelve years before that interview. Her mother was Métis. Her father worked in the saw mill. She was only eight years old when he left home. His departure was expected and even well-received. He had been offered a better job with another firm. "Supervisor," she was told. Frequently, at times twice per month, the cheques arrived. Then suddenly they stopped.

Her first impulse had been to run away from home and complete her own search for her father. Her mother was in no position to look. Most times she was drunk, or almost asleep in a depressed stupor. When it was learned that he had abandoned his wife, the number of their 'Ikwe' (care providers) suddenly increased. Everyone seemed related to everyone even though they were not all Métis. The local food bank was an absolute embarrassment, but they had to eat. Several men cut wood prior to that first winter so there was fuel for the metal stove. They barely survived. As weeks became months, all of the remorse was being expressed to her mother. That Karen was now without a father, no one seemed to care. Her hope for his return never died.

The supervisor was expecting her chest to explode with the redness of Karen's complexion. She returned to her story after collecting her thoughts. Then she described her schooling, her academic grades, and how she used school sports to mask the betrayal she felt. She had few friends and even fewer once the family's destitute condition was known. There was in fact an inverse relationship between her friends and government officials. As the former decreased, the appearance of the latter increased.

One of the government workers told her mother that she should not expect her husband's return. The manner of his departure continued to hurt them even more than news of his sudden death would ever have. Many men in the community worked in the mines, and unfortunately there was always the risk of fatal injury. Groups of other men worked on the bay. Ice, currents and waves could be equally perilous. "But to just leave!" Her mother constantly repeated the exclamation having been violated by her estranged husband's choice.

"Tom," he called himself with the initial introduction. Somehow he was associated with the government officials who were regular callers. He had a program for girls like Karen, and for youth wishing to become involved in sports. The play ground, behind one of the schools, was the venue for their activities. She was there among her classmates, and their presence always provided assurance.

Karen celebrated the return to baseball. Soccer too was invigorating. They were not exceptionally skilled. No one was, but they enjoyed themselves. The older boys and girls accommodated the younger ones. Winning was important but not essential. Participation was the key. If the federal government was trying to convince Canadians of the 'Participaction Program', Canadians had to look no further than that field in Thompson.

Of course it was beneficial that by early August, most of the mosquitoes had gone. That was one of the issues never considered for people fighting poverty. For them there was never enough money for repellants or pesticides.

Karen described herself as being devout. Her Métis mother continued the practice of her Catholic faith as often as she could. After receiving top marks in an arithmetic test, she was presented with a rosary from the parish priest. That relic still hung from the corner post of her wood-frame bed. With their church being named for St. Lawrence, Karen maintained a devotion to that saint. His feast day was August the tenth. She was also born on the tenth day of the month, but in January of 1959. The tenth day of every month was important to her. Good things always happened on the tenth day of the month.

It started raining during their baseball game on that tenth day of August. Some of the children left. Karen was so enjoying herself that she remained behind. When the downpour increased, the game was discontinued. The five children still there raced to Tom's vehicle. He took them home. Karen was the last child in the car, alone with the athletic group leader who had brought so much enthusiasm to her life. There, parked beyond a row of fir trees at the far end of the lot, she was introduced to the brutality of sex.

Karen went straight to bed after thoroughly washing herself. The stain suggested she had entered womanhood. Every time she wanted to talk about the incident, she stopped herself.

"Ladies should listen and not speak." Her mother's words from years before became vile, as if they were intended to always silence her fears.

It was well after ten o'clock before the employee interview concluded. Karen accepted the supervisor's ride to the far end of the city. The dark sky thick with ominous clouds suggested it might not have been the best idea to have her wait more than a half-hour for the next city bus. In the car, not a word was spoken. When the supervisor eventually arrived home, the explanation to his spouse was minimal. "Major meeting tomorrow," he offered.

The supervisor and employee said very little to each other for several weeks after that. On the first day, nothing was said at all. Simple greetings were the extent of their exchange for the next week. He wanted to help her more, somehow; but he was her supervisor and there were rules. Embarrassment forced her to say nothing more.

During that week, the supervisor spent lunch time hours in the library researching the basic information on Thompson, Manitoba. Therefore, if Karen ever mentioned anymore, her information might not radically shock him.

Thompson was known as the 'Hub of the North'. It was situated more than four hundred miles north of Winnipeg, and quite distant from Churchill on Hudson's Bay. The city candidly seemed too remote to offer any certain future. The alarming statistics concerning crime were degrading. Several articles suggested the city had the third worst crime rate per capita in

Canada. The major industries were mining, logging, and social welfare. Assistance was less than $150 per month in a setting when basic foods cost three to five times the price in the provincial capital. As a consequence of all the pressures and lack of any future, addiction was a constant social nightmare. The city even had to establish the position of "Community Safety Officer" to address the needs of the many who could not escape the realm of booze, drugs and poverty. The position's name alone spoke volumes of the dire needs.

Permanent jobs in established locations were extremely minimal. Government jobs or office positions existed, but these were generally occupied by many who were sent north from the provincial capital.

Thompson was called the 'Hub' because it was the focal point for so many aboriginal nations. Ten percent of the entire city was Métis. Twenty-five percent belonged to native tribes.

It appeared that every aboriginal community in northern Manitoba had a meeting house within Thompson. Thus, besides the Keewatin Nation, Thompson had become home to members of other tribes that included: Barren Lands, Brochet Community, the Cross Lake Band, Flin Flon Aboriginal, God's Lake Narrows, Island Lake, Keewatinowi Okimakanak, Mathias Colomb Band, Manto Sipi Cree Nation, Nikan Awasisak, Nisichawayasihk Cree, Norway House, O-Pipon-Na-Piwin Cree, Opaskwayak Cree, Red Sucker Lake, Sayisi Dene, Shamattawa, St. Theresa Point, Swampy Cree, Tataskweyak Cree, Thicket Portage Community, Waasagomach, War Lake Tribe, and York Factory.

The supervisor readily understood Karen's quandaries with respect to family life, the lack of hope and prospects, and how devastating the abandonment by a parent could be. They had little, and anything they lost became monumental.

It wasn't until the Thursday after Labour Day that they engaged in any meaningful discussion. "Making sauce this weekend," one of the employees mentioned before a team meeting. Karen knew all about that and eagerly joined the conversation mentioning how she used to do that with her mother. Interest was displayed when she talked about the different types of tomatoes and herbs they would use. Listening to Karen once more enthusiastically join a conversation was wonderful.

Days later in the cafeteria, the lighthearted conversation again returned. One of the employees had a jam sandwich. There was much ribbing as that person had always been prone to spend his lunch hours with adjusters or lawyers at some ritzy restaurant. The sight of jam cued Karen into the conversation where she described the various fruits and methods of making jams and preserves. Sugar was not so plentiful or economically feasible at the best of times, so having to use alternatives was a necessity. It was later that afternoon that Karen approached the supervisor and apologized for saying more than she should have. In turn he, as a friend not as a supervisor, offered his time and ears to her concerns.

It was in early December that she once again opened up with the rest of the story. She had tried a cautious relationship with one young man. However, that failed. She could not be free with her emotions and intimate expressions. "You can't escape your past," she confided.

Men would never again have their way with her. She convinced herself of that. She boldly advised that she never confessed the incident as sin because she was the victim. Karen added that immediately after the rape her energy disappeared, and was replaced with distrust, anxiety and recurring fears. Academic marks started to fail. She eventually was able to graduate from grade school, and barely made it into high school. With male teachers she was reluctant to participate. Women teachers were reassuring but they seemed to be looking through her. God was to blame at first. That attitude mellowed with time knowing that this 'Tom' was not doing God's will. Returning to the immediate anguish, Karen mentioned that during that first night she clutched her rosary and when the solace was not immediate she threw it in the corner.

Her openness on all of her past was becoming uncomfortable. Her supervisor was clearly assuming the role of her appointed psychologist. On one occasion just before Christmas she invited him and his spouse for dinner. She never forgot how to say, "Thank you."

It was abundantly clear that the issues she had with her aboriginal past were just as overwhelming as the sexual invasion. Karen asked about the parents of her supervisor and his spouse, ultimately adding that, "It must be so wonderful to have such good parents." That prompted her to immediately return to her mother's problems. Comments about her father concluded with her conjecture, "I still wonder if he's alive."

Karen repeated her personal history and all of the problems in the last years of grade school and throughout high school. She never attended any school dances and was most reluctant to engage in any social activities. When invited to participate in native gatherings, social events, or even just bake sales, she was at first most reluctant. It wasn't until the last year of high school that she realized there was some comfort in aboriginal activities. "They brought me home. I seemed to understand." Her words were simple regarding the positive effect of culture.

Although she lamented the limitations in their creative arts, participation was beginning to mean something. Trinkets, feathers, and wood carvings—these were all insignificant compared to the progress and commerce in Winnipeg. Taking the opportunity, she ventured with several students on a one-week outing. This was very much the last and only academic outing in her high school years. The trip on the Nelson River to the northeast toward Hudson's Bay was candidly most exhilarating. Her description years later conveyed such enthusiasm. That the leader and teacher was a woman was essential. The other five students were girls. She discovered more about herself, an independence that allowed her in part to escape her past. She proved to herself that she could do more than Thompson allowed her.

Late in the conversation, Karen expressed gratitude that she was an only child and figured that that fact contributed to her ability to avoid crime. She called crime a "family trap"; as if defending and supporting family members widened the web of illicit activity.

Her advice regarding employment was intriguing as she continued to ramble. When she talked of total loss automobile claims, Karen advised it was usual just to give the insured person cash and let him keep the clunker. In Thompson, there was one salvage yard and space was extremely limited. An insured person with several total loss claims on the same car was not uncommon. Evaluating native crafts that were stolen, burned, or damaged by flooding was becoming more difficult as prices were starting to escalate with the new tourist interest in native crafts. However the funds ended up in the pockets of the distributors—not the manufacturers or the vendors.

During the latter portion of the conversation that December evening, Karen lightheartedly talked about her future. At one point she seemed certain that she would visit her mother. That was just wishful thinking.

The New Year came, and the staff celebrated with an extra long weekend. The employees who combined those days with the Christmas holidays had not been seen for two weeks. Karen was not overly enthusiastic on that Monday, the fourth day of January. She walked into her supervisor's office and handed him a note. January 15TH would be her last day. She said she had a job with an insurance company in Toronto.

Regardless of any doubts anyone might have had, Karen talked highly of the prospect. For months after she left, queries about her produced the same repetitive response: "Haven't heard."

6

GERALD

"No!" His reaction was immediate. The insurance super-visor clutched the corners of the report and stared at the blank wall in disbelief. "It can't be!" His mind demanded the truth; but reality was not running away. It was right there in paper. The brief circumstances he knew from the preliminary report; but now the name. It stunned every sense. The victim's occupation was similar. "It can't be!" his furrowed forehead repeated the unbelievable possibility. He closed his eyes tightly, wishing he could reverse time and events: for them not to be there, or just for him to have said, "Don't do that. Stop for just one second. Don't go there."

Thoughts somersaulted with a dervish revelry tearing at every sense more with each moment. He reread the name. Nothing changed. Stone-faced with his chest pounding, he just for that minute closed his eyes. Thoughts of the past irrigated his mind, flushing the present reality with pleasantries of the past. Together they flooded the future within a realm that decreed, "Never again!"

The insurance supervisor hoped with every prospect that the victim was not his friend. How spiteful could God have ever been to provide the setting in which he would be the one han-dling the fatality claim of his childhood companion.

It was the autumn of 1982. The insurance supervisor had just visited the Norfolk County Fair. His firm had participated in the celebrations with a customer service stand. Being present in such communities was always beneficial for public relations. Although not absolutely acquainted with every avenue in that urban area, he was very much aware of the highway entering the city: one of the main access routes. Perhaps it would have been best in this case not to have any knowledge of the scene. However, being aware of such always added to the understanding of the circumstances.

He reread the details once more. This report provided specific information as to location and apparent action prior to impact. Scenes photos, the driver's statement, and a neighbour's evidence were added to the one page police report. That's all there was: no charges, nothing more.

A police cruiser struck a pedestrian who was pushing a wheelchair along Highway 3. The supervisor repeated to himself what had already been made obvious in the preliminary advice. He silently cursed the brevity of the independent adjuster's report, but knew he could not say more as that firm had a reputation for its quality judgements and detailed reports. Although it was the customary four pages in length with the additional attachments, the report seemed delinquent in essential details.

Questions as to why there were no charges seemed obvious. He pledged to clarify that situation: not in a chastising tone, but rather in a manner as if he was wishing to fortify the defence. His insurance company provided insurance for the province itself and for several municipalities. This was one of those cities. In reality his office insured the vehicle, the city that might have owned the property for any road allowance or a non-existent sidewalk, and the province that had control of the highway and owned the vehicle. If fault did not lie with one of his insured entities, then seemingly it could rest with another. Perhaps the independent adjuster realized this and decided to be brief so as to avoid playing one insured against another.

The failure to lay any charges was a benefit to the insurance company. It was indeed a rare occasion that a crown prospector would ever charge a police officer as a result of any motor vehicle accident. Evidence of impairment, excessive speed or gross.negligence would definitely be required. In this case there was none. Perhaps it was the erratic action of the person pushing the wheelchair that caused the accident. According to the adjuster, that seemed to be the case.

The supervisor returned his attention to the fatally injured individual. He was clearly the person pushing the wheelchair. The report advised he had been employed with a paraplegic association. The neighbour suggested she had seen him push that child back and forth to town on other occasions. The adjuster's report included one photo showing the shoulder of the road that was mainly loose gravel. The available sidewalk, according to the adjuster, was in disarray and torn up in the area of a new housing development. That forced pedestrians and bicyclists to the shoulder of the highway.

In spite of his supervisory role, he was always pursuing "the truth". That is how he described his position: one in which he weighed the evidence and only then made the decision. Two months before this occasion the supervisor had celebrated his tenth anniversary in the industry. He was not like his seniors who always seemed determined to take the easier path that was less complicated by all of the facts. He was also unlike the juniors who preferred everything to be so simple. "The truth," he whispered to himself while searching between the lines for what wasn't said.

"Where's the photo of the damaged wheelchair?" His notation was made on the side of page two. There was reference to the approximate cost, but common sense said that may not have been a basic model, especially if it was capable of being directed into town.

"Photos of the road: from a distance, at the scene of impact, and of the shoulder—where are they?" One was not enough. That was fundamental.

The final portion of the report once again raised the supervisor's temperature. "No evidence of liability." That conclusion was almost abhorrent. In Ontario, any driver striking a pedestrian is wholly liable for the accident unless he could prove the pedestrian's negligence. It was called the 'Reverse Negligence Rule'. How and why did that adjuster, so revered in the industry, reach his conclusion?

The supervisor paused, closing the report and leaving it front row and centre on his desk. A pile of files to the left corner would have to wait. His normal coffee break was no more than two minutes to grab a coffee from the dispenser and return to his office. Perhaps it was his facial expression or his manner that morning that prompted his staff to avoid him. Sitting once again in his office he perused the report.

"Gerald Taylor." The name was abundantly clear. The victim's birthday of April 14, 1947 was clearly evident. The supervisor repeated his ultimate wish, "It can't be." However, it was, but he refused to accept the obvious reality. Any ray of hope would help. Was there another person named Gerald Taylor with the same date of birth? The same occupation was another element that could not be discounted. Yet his mind was still racing for the possibility that coincidence did not definitely mean assurety.

The supervisor then telephoned the independent adjuster with a question he had never asked before: "Where is he buried?" His trembling hands did not rest while he waited for the return call.

The child's injuries diverted his focus only for a moment. The infant was eleven years old, known to be paralyzed from the waist down before the accident. His injuries were definitely severe, including fractured ribs, a rotator cuff injury and cuts and scars to his face, arms and chest. The wheelchair was basically demolished.

The immediate thought reflected the supervisor's compassion and understanding. "How much is a rotator cuff injury worth for an able-bodied person? How much is it worth for a child who requires both shoulders for mobility?" There would be serious discussions later on that claim's value, as there had been to that time no reported jury assessments with those specific circumstances. Candidly, no lawyer in his right mind would take such a case involving a paralysed child to a jury.

The probabilities, that his friend had died as a result of negligence by a person his company insured and that the file was on his desk, dumbfounded him no end. If this 'Gerald Taylor' was the same person who was his friend, the supervisor silently committed himself to doing whatever was necessary to make sure

Gerald rested in peace. The author shares this narrative having been the supervisor at the time with the insurance company in Hamilton.

We first met in September of 1958. I was at the time elated, as any nine-year-old would be, to attend my first altar boys' club meeting. It may be hard now to imagine a world where parents could trust their child to trek to a house about a mile away for a gathering in a basement. The home was occupied by the parish priests while the church and rectory were being built. The base-ment was one large room with painted walls and an area rug. There was a television, record player and a table with chairs. I had been an altar boy just four months before that occasion.

Gerald was there appearing very dignified even though he was just two years older. I immediately looked up to him for guidance and direction. There were other boys there, much older; but it was Gerald who had that helpful demeanour as he welcomed the younger altar boys into the activities or made sure they felt comfortable in spite of any shyness. There were more than twenty boys present on that first occasion. The number attending on the second Friday of every month for that first year continued to be approximately the same in spite of heavy snow or icy conditions. The priests always prepared snacks or mini-sandwiches. There were dart games with sticky nerf balls. Instruction was quick, and meetings usually lasted about an hour. Many of the boys also belonged to the Boy Scouts, so friendships were already shared by many.

For Christmas Midnight Mass, Gerald asked me to be one of the acolytes. That honour was much appreciated. After that we served many of the important occasions together. It was indeed a respect that filled my heart with an enthusiasm for everything spiritual. Serving daily mass, before school, became common place. Gerald did the same until September when he entered high school.

After school, chores around the church caused us to meet often. The priests relied on one of us to be present at all masses on Sundays in the event of emergencies. During the week we took turns cleaning the pews, sweeping the steps, or doing gardening chores. This was an age of spiritual vitalization where immigrants from every community in Europe had a special devotion for particular saints. Accordingly, preparations for such occasions were paramount. It meant so much for so many parishioners.

The chores around the church became rather multi-dimensional, even including bringing meals in sealed containers to the construction workers who were building the new rectory as well as to the shopping mall across the street. Men's and women's groups drew our attention, too, with their need to prepare the parish hall for their meetings. A simple expression of gratitude was basically the sole remuneration.

Gerald also developed a curiosity that summer with baseball, suddenly becoming quite excited about Warren Spahn and the Milwaukee Braves. He hadn't shown any real interest in the sport before then. However when Spahn recorded his 300TH win in August of 1961, he was most amazed. I never really understood his interest in that particular pitcher as Spahn was left handed and Gerald was clearly right handed in everything he did. Perhaps he was thinking of me.

In September of 1961, I entered grade seven in our parish school. Gerald at the same time was enrolled in the regional public high school. There was always quiet discussion about good Catholic students who would enroll in the public high school system. So often, the murmurs became ridicule.

I never questioned him. Even though we had known each other about three years, we rarely spoke of our family life. I was aware of his father and brother, but his mother was never mentioned. There was more than one occasion when I wondered what life was like without a mother.

It was just before Christmas that year that he called me to attend his house. I did so dutifully bearing in mind the sense of urgency that he conveyed. Gerald had been downtown picking up boxes of altar-bread for several parishes. "Can you deliver those to St. Edward's and St. Gabriel's?" After the affirmative response, I was on my way. At times my bike was my best friend.

At his home, Gerald had shown me his room. Behind the cross on the wall there were two eagle feathers. By the closet door a wampum belt was hanging, fully displaying the zig-zag pattern mixed with bright circles of coloured beads. A drum bearing an ornate skin occupied one corner of his dressing table. He had a strange radiance while I observed those relics of his heritage.

It was during the following Dominion Day weekend that he spoke more of his family. Gerald's father was "Indian." He then quickly added the term, "Chippewa." All of that at the time, in 1962, did not mean much. We lived in a multi-cultural community in north-end Toronto, so any reference to any cultural difference was insignificant in the broader picture.

Rumours started persisting about his brother who apparently "ran into trouble with the law." No one asked questions, but occasionally Gerald had to cut short his time with others to return home quickly.

Subsequent discussions revealed his father had difficulty keeping a job. He advised that his mother just left shortly after his fifth birthday. Gerald continued that subject by noting that his brother who was two years older took their mother's passing much harder. He then added that his father never recovered.

So often our conversations reflected his appreciation of God's grandeur. Everything about every aspect of nature drew his attention. I had no real appreciation of that sincerity at the time, other than to conjecture that perhaps he was keenly interested in botany or geography. Conversations eventually included the environment and ideas of worldwide catastrophe. National Geographic in January 1964 had released an article on the potential devastation that could be caused by Antarctica's melting ice. That prompted several more discussions.

Gerald's interest in creation embraced all phases. Whenever he chose to get a touch serious, the flow of the conversation would quickly turn to a series of queries concerning the fortune of the few at the cost of many. The inequality of wealth and distribution of assets were becoming more and more his main interests. In the course of one such discussion, he attributed his views to his native heritage. Such expressions began to give more meaning to the artifacts in his room. More and more he talked of sharing the wealth and assisting others. He was as much Chippewa as he was Catholic.

Gerald did not return to grade ten in the public school system. Instead, he entered the seminary in Chicago with the Scalabrini Fathers in September 1962. There he planned to complete the last three years of high school and spend one further year as a novice before becoming a religious brother. It seemed strange to me that he would consider an Italian-speaking religious order, bearing in mind his aboriginal heritage. However, it was the efforts of our parish priests that may have prompted the decision. They helped Gerald's father obtain a permanent job, paid for Gerald's tuition and were themselves members of the Scalabrini Order. When I last met Gerald that year on the Thursday before Labour Day, he was elated with the decision. I felt ecstatic for him because he was destined to succeed.

Distance interrupted the friendship for several years after that. Gerald would be home during the summers of 1963 to 1965. In that last year he spent just a few weeks in Toronto before attending the seminary on Staten Island for a week. That was planned to acquaint him with the residence for the coming year, while introducing him to working with the homeless and needy in mid-Manhattan.

By Christmas of 1965, Gerald was home. His father had taken ill, and his brother was nowhere to be found. Care providers were attending, not from the parish, but from a community north of Aurora. These persons would be later identified as being from the tribal community in the Barrie region. Specifics of who belonged to which tribe seemed to be becoming less important. All native issues at that time were considered generic matters involving persons belonging to one great big family under the auspices of Indian Affairs. It was truly these aides, attending to Gerald's father, who rekindled his trust with the native culture. Nothing was ever said until years later about any addiction to alcohol. Gerald cursed his father's habit over which his father had lost control. He let that be clearly known whenever he felt alone.

The thought that Gerald might abandon the religious brotherhood was becoming more probable with every passing week. He never returned to Staten Island and made it abundantly clear he would not do so while his father required his presence. In spite of this our parish priests offered him the opportunity to be a supervisor at the seminary's summer camp in July of 1966. The offer was also extended to myself and one other senior altar boy. The three of us readily accepted the chance to enjoy the highlights of New York, while considering the prospects we might still have in the religious life. That time passed quickly and was eventful especially for Gerald. Arrangements were made for him to continue his final year in the seminary. That his father had recovered, was dutifully abstaining from alcohol, and was with the intervention of the priests able to maintain his job, all these provided Gerald with the chance to pursue his own vocational goal.

In the late spring of 1967, my time working around the church was coming to an end. There were others similarly enthused to do the chores, while my school work needed more attention.

Meanwhile it was family matters that once again altered Gerald's intentions. His brother returned home. There was a fight. Gerald had to be there to intervene. At age twenty-one he was home once more to keep the slim chance of peace between his father and older brother. All that kept him going was his spiritual well-being that embraced his cultural heritage. On a couple of occasions when he had an opportunity to get away from home, he attended Martyr's Shrine as there was no other place that so closely aligned him with his father's ancestors.

With his main concern being the animosity and troubles within the family, Gerald relinquished his interest in the religious brotherhood and idea of serving the needy in some foreign country. Nevertheless, in his heart, he never abandoned the call to assist others. He entered the social worker program at Seneca College. With my acceptance to the University of Toronto and our individual academic workloads, we were basically destined to go our separate ways.

The Gasworks Tavern had become the author's inner sanctum. Situated near the university campus, it provided a refuge from the stress of exams, essays, and the world in general. Especially in the early summer of 1971, the meat pie with chips, gravy and a beer in the dimly lit confines was a feast away from the tribulations of street life. This was also my oasis during those months of helping the young teenagers escape the talons of their pimps. It was in that venue that I was suddenly shocked to see my childhood friend once more.

Gerald entered in black pants and a grey shirt. The dank coloured clothing was totally foreign in years past. His hair was considerably longer. His face was clearly marked by stress. Recognition wasn't instant. There's always the prospect of being mistaken. Gerald moved quickly to a table by the opaque window as if that was his regular spot.

After staring for a moment, while my meat pie got cold and the beer got warm, I got up and went over to his table. "It must be him," I thought as I ventured between tables. It was him.

The salutations were instantly exuberant. We recalled so much about the events in the latter years of the 1960s, including the serious moments. Gerald's father had passed away. I avoided any queries concerning his family. He did however offer that his brother ended up in jail, completed his sentence and entered rehab. After fifteen minutes the bartender brought me a new meat pie with a fresh beer. It was on the house. I had no idea Gerald had been a regular customer. He too received the same gratuity.

His questions about my university years followed. I provided information, but avoided any reference to the request by Hell's Angels to get the minors out of the strip clubs. As to why Gerald was downtown, the question was never asked. The thought was there however: "Did he ever complete his course?"

The conversation provided further details of Gerald's academic studies, advising that he had graduated and returned for an enhanced degree focussing on the needs of the homeless population. Urban street culture was to be the foundation of his final report necessary for graduation. He had until the end of August to submit same.

Even though he had conveyed such information, the author to that time was still unwilling to reveal details of his own involvement with the homeless young women. That matter remained concealed during the conversation that day.

After leaving the Gasworks, Gerald directed me to follow him from Yonge Street west for two blocks to Bay Street. There, across from the campus of St. Michael's College, we stopped. Gerald then invited me to observe those entering the book store. "This is a major problem," he blankly stated. His eyes remained riveted to the man wearing a trench coat in the late afternoon sun. I recognized him as a government manager. Later I was told that many government workers "are dependent on these stores." We parted company after an hour and pledged to renew our acquaintance.

That meeting did not occur for another week. We started our walk again from the Gasworks and returned towards the same book store. This time we entered. The musty odour was atrocious. The books on the shelves were all paperbacks, many were soiled or dog-eared. The cashier's counter was on the north side. Diagonally, behind the merchant, there was a curtain shielding an inner room from the general public.

Gerald walked directly to the east wall where he pulled a book off the shelf and forced it into my grasp. The cover clearly portrayed the name of a doctor and the title of his work. From cover to cover, in a series of seven chapters, it provided a vivid decree of incest involving minors. One didn't have to read anything more than the 'Summary of Chapters' page to discern as much.

"He's not a doctor. Checked. He doesn't exist." Gerald was extremely terse, bordering on being irate. Once outside, he advised that, "Nearly every book in there is like that, each one suggesting it's a psychological study on deviant behaviour." His frustration was clear. He deplored that our country, our province and our city were allowing such establishments to sell gross pornography under the guise of clinical studies.

He then directed me to a series of book stores on Yonge Street that, in the midst of all of the runaway teens, were selling magazines committed to the excitement of child pornography. Such graphic depictions were not hidden away, but rather they were available for anyone to browse or purchase. Proof of age was never asked.

Three days later we met again. This time I directed Gerald to the Zanzibar Tavern where he was shown the venue of my efforts. He candidly called me "a fool." The comment related more to the association with the bikers than any other aspect. He then called me "brave." There was a sense of respect, a sentiment we shared for each other's efforts and enquiries. From there the step was simple: I would share my research with him in order for Gerald to complete his detailed report.

Gerald had never taken this project lightly. He was determined not to just write about immorality or list the various stores and venues. Gerald committed himself to a complete analysis of the cause, the permissive nature of society, and the ultimate consequences. He wanted to prompt society and governments to act appropriately and close these venues of depravity.

Gerald started his analysis not with the adage that ignorance was bliss, but that ignorance was the consequence of comfort. "Why bother when it doesn't matter?" Accordingly he concluded that society, when it lacks understanding and knowledge, is never able to conjecture the consequence of any decision.

"When the benefits of life, liberty and the pursuit of happiness can be summarized as being 'permissive comfort'; then, society is exposing itself to perils it is unable to understand or control."

This freedom we claim as our privilege generates the expectation we can "observe and react while believing we can remain immune from the consequences of our actions."

"If he feels he is a victim of some ill-defined moral situation, then more than likely his audacity convinces him that everything is acceptable."

"If he firmly believes he is immune from the consequences, then his initial observation and continuing perception are morally supported by his initial judgement and continuing resolution."

"It then becomes a situation when perceived morality allows immorality. The desire to maintain satisfaction becomes a freedom just as much as life or happiness."

Gerald concluded that initial interest can ultimately become a repetitive action, becoming passion, and then with acceptance it all becomes an obsession.

At that point, compulsion is required to justify the continuing impulse, to the extent that the individual could possibly be considered no longer wholly responsible for any resulting crime. He never condoned any such activity, but saw the possibility that at some time society would wash itself of any involvement in the process of a person's demise toward immorality.

Also, one chapter was devoted to the horrendous attitude of society at the time, seemingly allowing child pornography and not preventing minors from becoming prostitutes. He asserted that that reality was known and those who were most in need or susceptible were not being protected.

Gerald's conclusion was simple: society had to do something.

On Wednesday, August the 18TH, that forty-two page report was completed. The report provided the addresses of sixteen bookstores and seven strip clubs involved in the pornography and prostitution activities. Four copies were collated: one for Seneca College, one that Gerald would keep, one for the police, and the last to be delivered to the Office of the Premier. The three deliveries were completed the next day.

Events followed quickly. Gerald received telephone advice that steps were already being taken and to do nothing more. There was another telephone call sternly advising to "cease and desist." Gerald was handed his diploma before Labour Day weekend.

Having completed that venture, we once again started to drift apart. We had been good for each other in matters in which we shared a mutual interest. After graduation I obtained employment in the insurance industry, meanwhile Gerald was gainfully employed with the paraplegic association.

Injuries as a result of a serious motor vehicle accident brought us together once more in the summer of 1973. His office was located in the city's east end. Our conversation was light and enthusiastic with each having much to say about the past. He was well-versed in all of the aspects of rehabilitation for the physically disadvantaged. Accordingly, Gerald was able to provide expert information on present equipment needs and the cost of future care. He was clearly at home in that venue with so many opportunities to assist so many individuals.

During our discussion, he was constantly being called upon for his advice. Once the telephone stopped ringing, there were knocks at his door. Trying to arrange any evening together was prevented by his calendar of endless meetings. He was booked solid every daylight hour for the next six weeks. We parted company for the last time that afternoon, although we had not intended it to be so. In spite of never meeting again, friendship remained eternal within the smiles of accomplishment.

The supervisor knelt before the grave of his dear friend. Brisk winds in mid November painted the solitary scene. All Souls' Day and Remembrance Day Masses had all been completed. The scent of incense no longer lingered among the floral displays. The surge of visiting families had already dwindled to just a few. Inspiring verses of sacred hymns floated across the grassy expanse echoing between the tombstones to rebound off the walls of the mausoleum. There was no actual music, just the impression of angelic hosts celebrating the accomplishments of the deceased.

He rose and stood there in silent respect for minutes more with his mind working overtime again wondering how he could assist someone, somewhere, somehow, to put forth the appropriate insurance claim for damages. Upon entering the grounds, the supervisor had asked the cemetery staff for information as to who paid for the grave, but that advice was refused. On one occasion years before, Gerald had mentioned a nephew—his brother's son from a common-law relationship. He didn't even know the child's name. Perhaps he was in his twenties. "Where was he?

Did he pay for the grave?" Or was it Gerald's derelict brother who suddenly turned good in a moment of need?

The supervisor left the cemetery that afternoon feeling very despondent. In all respects, he had tried. Perhaps someone visiting the plot would pick up the wampum belt that he left hanging by the grave marker. On the reverse side, he had fixed his business card.

He still visits the grave once every year to quietly reflect on Gerald's life: that his native heritage was so much a part of his spiritual and social accomplishments. The last phrase of Susan Boyle's 'Abide with Me' always joins the angelic chorus blowing with the wind beyond the expanse of willows and poplar trees across the wave of endless tombstones.

Hold Thou Thy cross before my closing eyes. Shine through the gloom and point me to the skies. Heaven's morning breaks, and earth's vain shadows flee. In life, in death, O Lord, abide with me.

7

ADONIO

The seventeen-year-old stared out the kitchen window, his eyes fixed to the enormity of the ice flow. As far as he could see, rough waters driven by the prevailing breeze swept sheets of broken ice from the west towards Buffalo. He had seen it every year, but never this much this early. In another month, or perhaps in just weeks, their journey over crests and through troughs would end, creating a formidable ice wall along the north shore of Lake Erie. Then like an invading monster from the glacial ice-world it was destined to cover the land: destroying docks, boathouses and shorelines.

Adonio was more than anxious as he awaited the telephone call. It was planned, not by him, but by a distinguished-sounding gentleman claiming that he required information regarding events over which Adonio had no control and candidly had little interest. The other person insisted they meet, but the teenager refused. He chose to talk at this time only because his parents would not be home. That would have to suffice. A beige-coloured telephone, secured to the wall, hung there in silence.

The teenager glanced around the room and peered into the den. It wasn't much of a room, but it always served the family's purpose. His parents didn't have many friends, at least ones that they would invite into their home.

Adonio always used the term 'parents' with grateful respect, bearing in mind George Smythie and his wife Tenia adopted him eleven years ago. So often he wondered what would have become of him if they had not been so charitable. Similarly he asked himself, but never his parents, as to why they even chose to adopt him. More than likely it had something to do with their inability to conceive. He had learned as much in his high school family life class. But in reality there seemed to be more than that because there was never any perception of reluctance or regret on their part.

Adonio was never shielded from his past. Everything about his natural parents was made known to him. In 1969, the love child was born to a Mohawk woman in the city hospital. For years she had avoided the reserve as if wanting to end all relationships with her past. His biological father had encountered grave difficulties maintaining employment and turned to substitutes to accommodate his personal failings. By the time he was two years of age, Adonio was receiving care exclusively on the reserve. The number of temporary guardians with so much abundant time was countless.

Then, out of the blue, this married couple in their thirties arrived expressing their intent to adopt a child in need. Perhaps it was his name that meant 'eagle', or his toothy smile. Whatever determined their choice made Adonio fly with joy among the eagles soaring free without borders.

Even as a seventeen-year-old, he still expressed every possible sign of affection and gratitude for each act of kindness. He was well fed and had countless opportunities to participate in sports, and enjoy the company of numerous friends. These were not all his student peers, but included neighbours, family friends and even a politician. He was never overtly close to any of these, but possessed a persuasive personality making adults wonder about his poise.

Adonio never forgot his heritage, and his adoptive parents were certain that would never happen. The belts, scarves, drum and relics were all symbols of his allegiance to the blood and community that gave him life. At least four times each year he'd return to the native environs, usually with his adoptive father, to share in celebrations and festivities. He had become a spokesman in his high school promoting improvements to the living conditions on the reserve. Twice the native community visited his school to celebrate the Spirit Circle.

Each evening he would, by memory, recite the Great Spirit's Prayer. The teenager obviously never knew Chief Yellow Hawk, but totally revered him as a saint. The prayer encompassed all of the spiritual and moral aspects of his being and culture. Adonio was so often prone to interchange the expression of 'self' with the term 'creation', because they were so much united in the Eternal Elder's great design.

Appearance-wise Adonio appeared to be native. His deep complexion and short-cropped hair suggested same. He loved bright scarves that were predominantly one colour. While others were adopting the new trend in turtlenecks, Adonio made sure his scarf was partly visible inside the collar of his shirt. He reserved the mix of colours for his wampum beaded-belts, one of which hung in his student locker.

He never begged for more. His parents always provided an abundant flow of assets to the extent his private bank account was never empty. Adonio knew full well that he was very fortunate in that regard. There was at least one annual major vacation. In recent years there were two. He tried dating on one occasion, but that never succeeded. The fault, as he perceived it, lay with him, as inherent pressures on teens led him to suffer ill-defined expectations. Perhaps he was too forward, or maybe she had issues with his lack of whiteness.

It was not yet four o'clock, and the sun was already setting behind the grey mass of distant clouds. In minutes, everything would be enveloped in a veil of black where shadows are afraid to roam. He abandoned the idea that that person would call. He had waited long enough. After closing the window shutters and then the blinds, he re-lit the potbelly stove. They had electrical heating and even an oil furnace, but a single log in the potbelly stove provided enough heat for those December evenings. After that Adonio sat on the couch to watch The Cosby Show and Family Ties. It was Thursday evening, and the kettle of water with the tea cups was on the counter awaiting his parents' return.

The choice was clearly his and the decision he concluded was most prudent. He chose not to make the call because he knew he couldn't rely on the evidence of a minor. The office clerk much preferred confirmation from the parents, but he realized that was not possible. They would not betray their confidence.

Representing the interests of Revenue Canada was not always easy. There was of course always the perception that their decisions were final and that people can't fight the government. Regardless of any such generalizations there remained the reality that this employee had principles. Those who willingly avoided taxes or chose to defraud the government in any way had to pay the price. The woman was his target. He was committed to get her, to stop her charade. But in doing so, he had to depend on reliable information. Truly, the minor's advice would not be enough to put her away.

Falcao eased herself from her satisfied employee. He was still smiling to himself thinking he was the world's greatest lover as she covered him with the soiled sheet. The East Asian woman was still active in her early fifties, accomplished in many tasks and adept in numerous trades. Her frail appearance deceived most into believing her capacity was suspect. She preferred it that way, realizing that her achievements were inversely proportional to their initial perception.

Harry would sleep soundly through the night. She was that good. It wasn't that she ever used sex to get her way. It's just that she used the talent that God had given her for her benefit.

Harry was his given name before she met him. Falcao first spotted the youth almost a decade before as he tried to impress as a barker at the Mud Cat Festival in Dunnville. The youth was clearly a failure in that chore. He appeared derelict and definitely in need of a good meal. She needed someone, particularly some-one who would obey her every whim and perform several chores not requiring any level of intelligence. She named him 'Ronkwe' meaning 'cleaner' in Mohawk. Falcao had no allegiance to any-thing Mohawk, it just seemed wise to do the little things to satisfy the native community. He would be seen as gainfully employed and she would be deemed to be a good person. To simplify his name, she called him Ronny.

Falcao returned to her own bed and to her husband. That she had just dutifully satisfied her employee didn't bother him

much, perhaps not at all. Stuart was an invalid. She preferred the term 'in-valid'. They had just celebrated his eightieth birthday even though he was much older. Because he couldn't remember anything meaningful, she called it his eightieth birthday just to celebrate an occasion that caused him to happily drool while trying to consume his cake. Clearly Falcao was perceived as a kind woman who lovingly continued to provide for her husband.

Privately she called him 'Estupro', a Portugese word meaning 'rape'. That was how they met in the weeks after the war in the western Pacific. A distinguished-looking combatant in an Allied uniform meant so much to any willing woman in the devastated countryside. Such a victorious soldier meant even more to the family of a young girl in similar surroundings. It was all about 'opportunity'. He possessed a higher rank, but his primal urge was no different than that of any infantry soldier. He celebrated with others, ultimately taking the virginity of a young woman whom he thought was at least eighteen. She was only twelve. The 'sex card' was played to perfection, and a month later she was on her way to Canada as his wife.

He chose not to return to the hell he left behind during the war. His first wife had already procured a lover. The divorce from the prestige-grabbing woman was quick. However, the vixen he had been forced to marry in the Far East ultimately proved to be no different.

The mood at breakfast was extremely tense. Obviously his parents once again did not agree. Adonio cowered away from these silent moods as if he was able to recall every moment of discord between his natural parents. "Just don't fight," he quietly begged his parents. They didn't fight, at least not in front of him. Instead they just remained hushed, a silence that echoed throughout the house. After his father left to clear the dusting of snow from the walkway, his mother revealed the issue. In three days time they could take another vacation. One of their customers had, as she had done in the prior two years, offered a trip for a week to a Caribbean resort.

"What's wrong with that?" Adonio's silent self-expression was immediate.

Tenia however was not your simpleton. There were issues she told herself. "We won't be bought!" she had already exclaimed to her husband. She was definitely more pragmatic. Her husband tended to act on a whim, being at times overly infatuated by the 'freebees' their industry generated.

Tenia's parents died approximately eight years before. With that unfortunate event, the only child, Tenia, received a magnanimous estate. Immediately, with outrageous interest rates approaching twenty percent, she turned that inheritance into an even greater profit. Anyone's simple request for a loan after that became the foundation for their family business. They were not just the investment advisors, they became mortgage lenders.

The woman, that Tenia called the 'Falcon', was their major client. It started with one loan that became liens on four properties. Tenia never trusted the Falcon. To start with: she was obviously East Asian, known to be an immigrant, married to a distinguished member of the military that no one ever saw, and able to purchase questionable properties and businesses from which she always generated a significant profit.

There were other matters that caused grave concerns. Tenia deplored the reality that that woman used the Portuguese language as if to disguise her persona and most likely her intent. She had heard the name, Estuprador, that the woman called her elderly husband. "How can I trust any woman who calls her husband a rapist?"

Tenia, during conversations the prior evening, was informed that "The Falcon Lady" wanted strippers in her bar, and that the regional bikers objected unless they shared in the proceeds, and more particularly that the application for the general entertainment license was rejected by city council. With that information alone, that woman had obviously played all of her cards. "Obviously not a poker player," Tenia had told her husband.

By the time his father finished shovelling the snow, the temperament inside the house returned to normal. Adonio was told about the offer for a vacation on the twenty-second of the month, in four days' time. He was delighted. That was more than enough to ease the tension, even though Tenia continued with her suspicions. "What's going to burn this time?"

The first two buildings that burned to the ground were insured by another company. Falcao deliberately chose another insurer for the third hotel. Everything seemed to be working so easy for her, at least until city council denied the strippers. If she needed a loan, she got it. If insurance was necessary, there were no problems. If the Crime Prevention Bureau should have had notice of the first two fires, it didn't. If she needed illegal liquor in plastic bottles from the States, there was no delay. As a consequence of false ledgers, concealed income and fraudulent tax returns, an audit was never finalized.

Ronny was her tool, although she treated him like an employee. Whatever she wanted, he was there for her. If anyone ever accused her of arson because of exclusive opportunity, Ronny possessed the second set of keys. She gave to charities, provided her venues for fund raising, and supported regional sports. That some of the athletes used her buildings for the source of their addiction was no one's business.

Falcao had, prior to 1986, escaped all detection and had suitably profited from her arson adventures. In each case, she had made necessary enquiries and arrangements to assure herself quick profits. Regarding the first building, she purchased same for about twenty-five per cent of its replacement cost. To secure an outrageous figure for the replacement cost, she purchased the expertise of a property appraiser with favours and blackmail. He was so impressed that he stayed on board to repeat similar activity for her next two buildings. With the inflated figure for the replacement cost, she then approached the Smythie's who were at the time looking for investment customers. Her request to them was simple: her assets plus their loan had to equal eighty percent of the replacement cost. That way she'd be assured of replacement cost and their investment would be secure.

For reasons unknown except to those planning arsons, there was a rule pertinent to the handling of fire loss claims that said: if the owner was determined to be the arsonist, then the mortgagee still had the right to recover its financial interest. The extrapolation to that was: if the insurance company is compelled to pay the mortgage company its portion of the settlement funds, then the insurer has the right of recovery against the arsonist. In all that, the owner-suspected-arsonist still had the right to file his or her own Proof of Loss form and then commence litigation.

With the first two buildings there was no accusation of arson, and the Smythie's appropriately recovered the amount of their lien. That those two fires occurred between Christmas and New Year's when the firefighting force was barely staffed—one in 1984 and the next in 1985—had Tenia absolutely concerned about what might happen when her family was scheduled to be away in Jamaica.

The Caribbean waves were rough that Christmas morning. Regardless of the sun and pristine beach in the all-exclusive resort, Tenia remained apprehensive. She tried displaying a sense of enjoyment, but found that disguising her true feelings was becoming increasingly difficult.

Adonio could easily sense there was something that was just not right. His parents never mentioned anything specific while they were away. However, he readily conjectured that it had something to do with the scant pieces of information he received the week before.

The New York Giants won the Super Bowl on January 25, 1987 by defeating the Denver Broncos 39 to 25. The victory had been declared even before the kick-off. The pundits were absolutely certain. Similarly, Falcao was certain of her venture. The fire had been set and less than two days later relit. The police and fire department had attended on both dates. The investigation was undertaken, and her initial Proof of Loss form was filed.

The twenty-sixth of January was the thirty-third day following the first fire. The Falcon Lady's luck was about to change. On that morning, the claim file in its entirety was transferred to the author. In his capacity as a senior claims specialist, he was asked to handle the matter to its conclusion.

Everything described or conveyed in the context of this narrative is determined from first-hand involvement, personal enquiries, expert reports, available evidence all deemed to be the truth. The reliability of any second-hand information and opinions expressed by various persons has been supported by other sources. Names are changed because of the suggestion of a criminal act. No charges were ever laid and no criminal act ever proven in court. However, when you stare at four aces in your hand, you know you are holding four aces.

Falcao had insured the wooden structure with a replacement cost of two million dollars. My insurance company was lead insurer on a subscription policy involving many other insurers.

Whatever decision we made, the others would follow. On the day the file was reassigned, all of the insurers had already concluded the owner was responsible for the arson.

Getting to that conclusion was easy. The initial fire started inside the premises, specifically behind the bar after 6pm on Christmas Eve. No one was inside at the time. To that point, it appeared Falcao had the only set of keys. One bottom window was broken, with glass chards outside the building meaning the window could have been used to escape, not to break in. Inside the premises, the safe was open and financial records had been doused in gasoline. Behind the bar, the remnants of plastic American jugs of liquor had fallen to the floor.

It was a three-alarm blaze. By four o'clock in the morning the fire had destroyed the building, so much so that it could not have been rebuilt using the existing foundation. Because there was a chance of embers reigniting in the breeze and without snow or rain expected, there was a guard assigned to protect the site. During the evening on Christmas Day someone attended to dismiss the guard. The remaining structure was ablaze early in the morning of Boxing Day. Authorities again attended. The building was completely levelled.

An arsonist counts himself lucky escaping the scene after the initial blaze. No civic authority could recall any incident when an alleged arsonist returned to rekindle the blaze especially when there was not much left to be ignited.

The independent adjuster's first two reports told a wonderful tale of how simple it would be to prove the building owner was responsible for the fire. However, there were no photos of the glass chards, and there was no signed statement from the building owner. She had refused to provide one after allegedly receiving advice from her counsel.

My first call was to the adjuster regarding the woman's potential involvement in other fires. He said that he had spoken with the Fire Marshall's Office and that to that day there had been no record of other fires involving this insured person. We needed that evidence. It seemed there were two possibilities: either the prior insurance companies didn't file reports with the Insurance Crime Prevention Bureau, or the building owner was using another name, perhaps an Ontario Limited Numbered Company. In any event, three months later after Falcao became aware of the issue, reports on the first two fires seemingly made their way to the ICPB indicating the building owner was not suspected in those claims.

There was not much to see at the scene. The safe was extracted from the premises by crane, and the contents were seized by the Fire Marshall's Office. After that they were sent to Revenue Canada who had, prior to the fire, commenced their own investigation. It was affirmed that the business records were covered in gasoline, so much so that all of them could not have burned. The safe had to have been opened by someone knowing the combination as there were no signs of tampering. By mid April, Revenue Canada determined that Falcao owed the government more than sixty thousand dollars in back taxes. It then decided the government would not charge the owner for tax evasion until the insurance companies were finished with their claim. If the insurers paid the loss, there would be no tax evasion charges.

The Equifax report, completed in conjunction with her application for the strippers three months before the fire, affirmed she had no financial motive at that time to collect insurance proceeds. The adjuster then discussed the matter with a city councillor who suggested her financial situation was not that solid. The Falcon Lady had recorded the mortgage loan from the Smythie's in the name of her husband alone even though Smythie's copy of the actual documents conveyed her sole participation in the loan.

The insurance companies' argument with respect to exclusive opportunity took a hit the moment Ronny signed his statement indicating he too had a set of keys, and that there was a third set. However he did not know who had that third set. In other words, anybody could have found that third set and gained access to the building on Christmas Eve. Ronny's statement included a list of his many chores, clearly reflecting he was overworked and at times not always reliable. He admitted that it was possible that he left the building unlocked. The weakness of the statement lay in his testimony that he returned home after leaving the premises on Christmas Eve and that he did not see the building owner until after Boxing Day. But he lived with The Falcon Lady.

By the end of April, 1987 the Fire Marshall's report was still not complete; the Crime Prevention Bureau had not finished its investigation; the fire department had completed its report without the benefit of statements from the attending fire-fighters; the police simplified its process without all of the statements. Unfortunately the investigation upon which a denial could be sustained in court was never fully completed. Evidence went missing in the first days, and everyone had jumped to conclusion about Falcao's guilt, ultimately seeming to believe nothing more had to be done. It didn't matter how many questions I had, or how many more suggestions were posed, not everyone was marching to the same tune.

Having denied her claim asserted on the Proof of Loss, she instituted action against us. Each insurance company was also being sued for punitive damages that could potentially double the award.

It puzzled me in this case that the mortgagee who had a lien of five hundred thousand dollars never filed its own Proof of Loss for that amount. That would have been a slam dunk. The mortgagee's omission prompted our second meeting with our own lawyer. If we pushed the mortgagee to claim $500,000, then we might be inviting both the mortgagee and owner to join forces. If they remained apart, the mortgagee's evidence could be helpful in our defense. If we didn't instruct the mortgagee of its right to make a claim for its interest, then we might be acting in bad faith.

Also, we discussed replacement cost and actual cash value figures. We determined then that the cash value of the original structure was in the realm of $300,000. The replacement cost with all of the upgrades to meet the building code would be about $1,000,000. She clearly over-insured the building. With adjusters from the other insurance companies present, our lawyer announced he was all gung-ho to proceed with the defense. Afterwards he spoke to me privately, being quite terse: "You've been ambushed."

After that meeting, enquiries to the building appraiser who had suggested two million dollars for the replacement costs could not be answered. His business was closed.

By the end of the summer, the fire fighter, who was to testify that the glass chards were in the dirt outside the building, changed his story suggesting that the glass may have been on the basement floor. That meant the window was a means of ingress, not egress.

City hall granted Falcao's application to rebuild.

The police notes were never transcribed and some remained illegible.

There were no subsequent demands by Falcao's legal council to pay the claim. She was clearly conveying the perception that she was in no rush for the settlement funds. Persistent demands tend to be common for those who are worried about the weaknesses of their cases.

Everything was looking dismal for our defense, and then we received a call from the Crime Prevention Bureau. Ronny was changing his story.

Within seventy-two hours, he was completing a sworn affidavit stating that Falcao told him exactly what to say, specifically that there were only two sets of keys and that at all times he had one of those with him. She had concocted his lies.

The Crime Prevention Bureau added that it had conferred with Revenue Canada. Falcao's indebtedness for back taxes under her name alone exceeded $120,000. Further enquiries were being made under other potential names and businesses.

Further, the bikers, Satan's Choice who controlled such affairs in lower Niagara peninsula, advised they would never have allowed her to have strippers in her club even if city council had agreed to same.

Financially her hotel and its bar were destitute. Former customers were willing to testify that there were no more than twenty customers on any given day.

It was looking good.

The news of the jockey's death stunned George Smythie. He had heard the rumour several times that a jockey must have been involved in the burglary at the time of the fire. Falcao had been the first to mention that prospect. The basement window's size would have prevented a person of regular height from using the window to break into the basement. There was another aspect too that worried him about a jockey being mentioned, for George had already been told by other second-hand sources that several athletes and students were using the hotel as their source for narcotics. That particular jockey had been the subject of suggestions of illegal substances. Having already completed the mortgage transaction, George was to say the least more than a trifle worried about his investment.

Equally demanding his immediate attention was advice to the police that a blue Comet vehicle had been seen leaving the property after the jockey's murder. Smythie owned a blue Mercury Comet.

He had already told the adjuster in a sub-rosa meeting that he would not under any circumstances complete their own Proof of Loss form for the amount of the mortgage. He'd give up $500,000 just to get away from her.

The longer that the litigation dragged, the more uncomfortable George and his wife became. Actually, the legal process was not delayed at all. The Discoveries were already scheduled for February of 1988, just nine months after Statement of Claim was delivered. Still, for George any time period under the circumstances seemed just too long.

The Fire Marshall's Office had, by the end of August of 1987, completed its report. Nothing more was going to be done at that point in time. However, the FMO would recommence its investigation if the Discoveries produced information that prompted it to consider further avenues.

From the distance the adjuster spied on George and Adonio as they celebrated with the native community. The lacrosse game would become the focus of their attention in the late evening. However, in the mid afternoon they danced and chanted until all present encircled their chief in celebration. Representatives of all of the community's departments and offices participated in those festivities. Women too were busy with the artifacts and relics, their cooking and hand-made clothes. This was their show of allegiance and their commitment to their future as one in common practice and determination. The Spirit Circle encompassed more natives than Adonio could have ever imagined. His father had no reservations about participation, and did so with earnest enthusiasm. This was becoming a part of his son's life, because this was his son's heritage.

The adjuster missed his opportunity on that occasion to talk to either Adonio or his father. After an hour he left realizing his ability to gain new or usable information had vanished. He would prepare himself for the Discoveries in several months' time. Until then the denial of coverage would be maintained.

There were no fires to any of Falcao's building between Christmas and New Year's Eve in 1987. She continued to display the image of an elderly feeble woman plagued by the false accusations of her insurance company. Meanwhile, away from the public's view, she remained conniving and forceful to the extent fears were becoming all too real among those who knew her personally or through business.

The Falcon Lady really had no reason to be too worried about any litigation. Although this was just a civil matter, the lack of criminal charges spoke volumes of the government's inability to prove its case. The extrapolation for her lawyer was simple: if the government can't prove she started the fire, then how is the insurance company going to succeed? The cold hard reality included: there were no criminal charges accusing her of arson; there was no demand by Revenue Canada to pay back taxes; and all of the suspicions by the Fire Marshall and the Crime Prevention Bureau did not produce any firm allegation, just a lot of innuendoes. However, Falcao had to be in total control, and vowed that would remain her modus operandi.

The sheepish voice begged to speak. The telephone conversation took place in the first week of January. That is usually one of the busiest times in the claims department: after the two long weekends and inevitability of speeding drivers on icy streets trying to get to holiday destinations as quickly as possible. The norm is to rush such discussions so as to keep as many customers satisfied as possible. However, in this case, rushing the matter was not an option.

The caller identified himself as Adonio. I was glad he called. "I need to speak to you," he continued. Twenty minutes later the conversation concluded. His primary interest was fear for his parents. When asked to advise the reason, the teenager stated candidly that, "The woman had the jockey killed." He was obviously relying on hearsay opinions because the police had never reached that conclusion. The death was still being called, "Suspicious." I was careful what I said realizing that Adonio might just repeat a version of what I said to others. More importantly he timidly implored my help, "If you can." I offered as much assurance as I could, knowing it would never be enough. Adonio tried to tell me about his parents' business. He was only repeating what I already knew. "Never get involved with her," he wished. I let him proceed because he definitely was a young person in need of an ear.

We also met right after work the next day as he had requested. So much of what he had already said was just repeated in person. Ultimately he got to his primary point. He wanted to see my facial expression and hear my words. I promised to leave his parents out of the issue for as long as I could. He didn't really favour that advice and stared straight at me without saying another word. He then heard me say that I could not make any promises because so much depended upon The Falcon Lady and the lawyers. Was his parents' evidence required to confirm Falcao's involvement in prior arsons? More than likely it was. Still I said what he wanted to hear, and he left satisfied.

I never told our lawyer about this meeting or any of my personal enquiries or activities. He had the police, reconstruction engineers and the expert firms on which to rely. I didn't want him hearing too many opinions or suggestions and potentially using them as being the absolute truth. Further he was representing ten insurance companies on the subscription policy. I heard the interests of a select few persons and maintained their confidence.

Anyone undergoing the process of Examinations for Discovery is indubitably going to be at least slightly apprehensive. The adjuster was extremely so on that February morning. The only calming aspect was the fact that he knew Falcao's lawyer. That attorney was a gentleman in other matters and candidly was expected to be so in this case. I had rehearsed every aspect at least six times making sure that I would never mix reality with suggestion as there had been so many incidents and varying reports in the last fourteen months.

Surprise was the reaction with less than five minutes of questions. The Falcon Lady's lawyer limited his questions to confirmation of the policy coverage, initial-notice of the fire, date the Proof of Loss form was received, and the date coverage was denied. He never asked why we were denying coverage as the Statement of Defense had clearly established the reason.

Before leaving the room, the lawyers talked off the record about their plan for the rest of the morning, that being Ronny's Sworn Interrogatory. Because he had produced two statements, the latter incriminating Falcao, they wanted his evidence under oath on the court record. Together the three of us headed to the waiting room.

We stopped dead in our tracks. The Falcon Lady was sitting there facing us. She was not to have been there because her discoveries were not scheduled until March. She rose smiling. It is hard to say it was an evil grin because I had never met her before. Defense counsel no doubt immediately thought it was inappropriate for her to even be there. She spoke to her lawyer. His expression became ghostly white.

Our lawyer asked the receptionist if Ronny had arrived. Her answer didn't please him.

The Falcon Lady's lawyer then called our defense lawyer aside. They were in a private room for more than five minutes. When they left, our lawyer's face was beet red. Obviously he was extremely irate. After taking me back to the discoveries room he said, "He's dead."

Shock was total with the news that Ronny had died the night before. Of course our defense on the argument of exclusive opportunity had also just died.

Back at our lawyer's office, our counsel asked his assistant to adjourn Falcao's discoveries. He then closed his office door and sat me down with a stern expression. His tone was serious. "How much is your life worth?"

I didn't answer.

He stared at me.

I pulled a quarter from my pocket and flipped it. When placing it on his desk, I declared, "Heads." I then ended the meeting by telling him I'd be back to him "next week."

Before that happened, actually on the fourth morning after my discoveries, I received a call from the police officer who had been given control of the closed investigation. Ronny had just been discovered floating in the Welland Canal.

The Falcon Lady knew of his death three days before the body was discovered. She had never at any time reported him missing. Suddenly she was suspected of murder, not just of arson and drug dealing and tax evasion.

Adonio called me just before Christmas in 1988. The nine-teen-year-old was on his university winter break. He was abso-lutely elated not only with the settlement but in the manner we were able to protect his parents. That alone relieved so much of his stress. His comments revealed that Falcao's plotting had involved members of the aboriginal community. However, none would ever admit to it.

There was not a stone she left unturned. Every possibility of complicating our defense by having parties and persons con-found each other, she accomplished. Ronny was dead, but there was no proof that Falcao caused his death. The evidence that she started the fire could be challenged. There remained no charges relative to the arson, drugs or tax evasion. Either everyone was totally afraid of her, or they were grossly incom-petent. Even Falcao's lawyer admitted later that he had "his doubts."

The other nine insurers remained squeamish. Even though among them they shared eighty percent of the risk, there was no decisiveness. They all continued to state that they would just go with the decision of the lead insurer who had twenty percent of the risk. The process of negotiations rested with myself.

Our first offer was $500,000 that matched the amount of Smythie's loan.

Her delay was atrocious. She had expected $2,000,000 plus interest and an award for punitive damages, and so she displayed no inclination to budge. In fact she chose not to respond as she felt the insurance companies would make a better offer before she even had to decline it. It was her way, outside of the violence, that she conducted business.

Our second offer was $600,000.

She finally countered at $1.75 million.

Our third offer came in at $700,000.

She answered by asserting that we only went up $200,000, whereas she had already dropped more than $250,000.

We then stalled to disturb her even more. At the beginning of November, five months after our first offer, we tabled what we described as, "Our final offer of $750,000 all inclusive of all costs and legal fees." We sensed her lawyer wanted to get paid and get her out of his life.

That offer would have broken down in this way: $500,000 to her mortgage company, at least $80,000 for legal fees, and less than $170,000 in Falcao's pocket.

In mid December that offer was accepted, and the release was signed in exchange for the settlement cheque prior to Christmas.

The following August, Adonio asked me to meet him at the Six Nations Festival. He wanted to personally express his gratitude that the case had been resolved, and that his parents were spared. Smiling, he declared his pride in "the achievement that's possible when people work together." Such expressions were heartwarming as none of the insurance companies including my own employer, our lawyer, the police and all of the authorities had ever expressed their gratitude.

Hearing the beat of drums and chant while watching the colourful dance and attire during all of the celebrations was inspiring as much as it was spiritual. Adonio remained true to the wisdom of his heritage, and to his family and community. The young man would no doubt continue to excel in life with his foundation remaining solid in indigenous culture.

1991

REV. JAMES TOPPINGS

The impassioned verse of Lieutenant Colonel John McCrae's poem gripped the hearts of many Canadians during the Christmas season of 1915. Ypres was a distant field in a far off land, unknown to many, yet it had become the muddy tomb of more than eight hundred thousand souls. Prime Minister Borden, into his fifth year of leadership, was quite unable to extricate the nation from such devastating carnage. Throughout the country, poverty and recession held hands down the aisle of diminished expectations. The issue of conscription was about to ignite hostilities in Quebec. In Southern Ontario, residents were about to experience a new scourge: Le Club de Hockey Canadien who were about to win their first Stanley Cup.

Within an improvised cubicle of Verdun hospital's maternity ward, James Toppings was born on January 16, 1916. Ten weeks later the Montreal Canadiens won the championship and thus began the foundation of his ardent affair with his most-favoured team.

His was a loving family with parents who provided a quality Christian lifestyle based on hope and charity. The expansion of his parents' trust was grounded in their faith knowing that the virtues they instilled would never be brushed aside by frivolous temptations. Sunday Mass with frequent reception of the sacraments enhanced the young boy's spiritual life. Pilgrimages to Trois Rivieres, Quebec City and Beaupre increased his enthusiasm for Catholic practice.

At age twelve, James entered Loyola High School. His classmates were predominantly bilingual. Being absolutely conversant in two languages opened many opportunities not only in school but throughout life. Acquaintances were not limited by ethnic background once additional linguistic skills were mastered. High school thus became the forum where James developed his love for languages, history, the classics and of course religion.

After graduating from high school at age sixteen in June, 1932, James spent the next year working odd jobs and doing as much as possible to put food on the family table. The Great Depression had ripped every segment of society apart. Jobs were scarce and pay was pitiful. Surviving on one family income was not possible.

The following July he entered the novitiate in Guelph, Ontario, and two years later took his preliminary vows. His time there introduced James to new ethnic cultures: the German, Dutch, Amish and Ukrainian. He became part of their communities as much as he could, while enjoying the venues of St. Jacob's, Elmira, and Kitchener. Similarly he discovered his love for the outdoors and took every opportunity for long treks and even paddling. Witnessing their community efforts to ensure a quality life for everyone became, for James, a vision of God-among-men. All were considered equal within their community and beyond their normal parameters. Amish buggies on their way to the market, Ukrainian children in play grounds, and multi-ethnic sports teams: all of these simply affirmed that life was just not English or French or even just both.

After taking the initial vows, James began an earnest study of classic literature: Greek, Roman and medieval. This was not confined to just the normal texts, but included rare editions. Once again his understanding expanded with Middle Eastern, East Asian and Norse culture.

The multi-ethnic experience continued in Toronto during his three-year course at the Jesuit Seminary. There he freely acquainted himself and enjoyed the company of so many from the Greek, Polish, Italian, and East Asian communities. The world was becoming so small while the compulsion to embrace it was ever more increasing.

In the year after the war started, James having graduated from the philosophy program returned to Montreal to teach at his old alma mater, Loyola High School. There he taught languages, found his niche with Grade Nine students, and coached football and hockey teams. The Montreal to which he had returned was significantly different from the city he left just six years before. It had become a cosmopolitan centre for immigrants fleeing the torment and tribulation that had been sweeping every grain of life out of Europe. High school was no longer just fluent French Canadian students. Many languages were spoken in the hallways, making some aspects of communication a sincere challenge. James learned patience.

Returning to his ultimate dream to be ordained, James completed the three year theology program and was ordained by Cardinal McGuigan in Toronto on June 30, 1947.

That same summer following the Indian Independence Act of July 18, 1947, Reverend James volunteered to teach at the Darjeeling Mission in northern India. This was a school in the North Point community lodged between mountains in the Southern Himalayan Range. The community lay north of Bangladesh (East Pakistan at the time), and was about 100 kilometers from the Bhutan border to the east. Delhi was 1,400 kilometers to the west. The academic institution was established by the Jesuit Order in 1888 and remained committed to ensure excellent education and opportunities for young people. It was with much enthusiasm that Reverend James anticipated acceptance. Unfortunately, that was not the will of his superiors. The same internal ailments that affected his health less than a decade before were considered a significant obstacle to his wellbeing should he be stationed in a remote community without adequate emergency health care. Reverend James was returned to Loyola High School the following year where he became the school's Vice Principal.

While in that position, Reverend James completed his tertianship, which is a period set aside for spiritual retreat by a seminarian or priest to contemplate his complete commitment. Following that, Reverend James achieved his education degree, and was then assigned to St. Paul's College in Winnipeg. He served that academic community for eleven years from 1952 to

1963. During that time, Reverend James also completed his Master of Arts degree.

It was during his tenure at this college school that Reverend James employed his abilities in a multi-ethnic setting, addressing the various concerns and needs that could never be scripted before the morning sunrise. He remained teaching the initial year of high school providing a more than adequate introduction to the various stress factors that any young man would experience in those formative teenage years. Unfortunately school boards were still so committed to guaranteeing that no element of anxiety ever befell any grade school student. The task then fell upon the grade nine teacher to counsel and advise the students regarding tension they had never before experienced. The first impression of any student remained consistent: that grade nine teacher really cared.

Reverend James was considered even more important by those students who were not part of the cultural majority, or who viewed themselves as not belonging with the rest. Although St. Paul's College was a private boys' school, not all of the student-population was white English speaking. Winnipeg demographics were significantly diverse with only 55% identifying themselves as English, Scottish or born-Canadian. Approximately 12% of the population was predominantly French-speaking. The ethnic communities included: Ukrainian, German, Italian, Polish, Irish and Filipino. With all of these nationalities, Reverend James was acquainted with their customs and expectations. He was prepared to assist them where he could.

Then there was the aboriginal community whose numbers exceeded 10% of the city's population. In Toronto, and to some extent in Montreal, their culture had been assimilated into the larger framework of the English-speaking population. However, in Winnipeg, there was a significant difference. There was definite reluctance to relinquish native identity. That tribal pride remained firm, urging aboriginal persons to never forsake their past. Reverend James had learned so much in Montreal and elsewhere in his personal development. Freely he accepted the challenge to accommodate all of the varying needs of these indigenous young men.

Accordingly, Reverend James acquainted himself with Cree and Métis expressions. His attempts in their languages caused many to laugh. The fact that many of the aboriginal students were totally bilingual brought them closer to the virtues of their teacher. They affirmed that he was one of them especially in the ability to diminish life's anxieties by unexpected moments of laughter.

Communication and academic lessons were not his only interest when considering the students from the aboriginal communities. He actively supported the bursary program necessary to fund the tuition for native students. School uniforms were required, and no aboriginal student or any young man in need went without proper attire.

Sports remained an after-school specialty. Reverend James was annually coaching football, or track teams. Of course there was also hockey. Needless to say, members of the hockey team shook their heads when Reverend James jokingly suggested they should don the jerseys of the Montreal Canadiens. Of course, if they said 'yes' then he wouldn't have been jesting.

The longer he taught aboriginal students the more and more he became involved with their interests. His concern was not just answered by prayers but rather in one major case by action. Reverend James was shocked that so many young girls and boys were being removed from their native communities based on the perception that these children would have a better education and life elsewhere. They were being dispatched throughout Canada, and also to the United States and even to Europe and Australia. This was totally abhorrent and prompted many discussions among the other teachers and with the Rector of the college. Ultimately, he pledged his assistance to the campaign to stop the dismemberment of native communities.

The author first met Reverend James in August of 1963, just weeks before starting high school at Brebeuf College School. On that occasion, I was delivering altar bread from the Sisters of the Precious Blood to the various churches and religious institutions in the North End of Toronto. My first impression echoed what others had said in the past and what many more would say in the future. Reverend James Toppings was a wonderful person.

The comments that are included here repeat the context of various personal conversations. Reverend James treated students as equals, making it so easy to converse with one so well regarded. Together with the elderly Rector and another priest Reverend Donald Beaudois there were many during-and-after-school discussions regarding perceptions about life in general. Reverend James never wavered from his beliefs, maintaining the principles that made his life virtuous. The concept of 'Freedom of Conscience' was introduced to us, but at the same time his opposition to birth control and abortion remained firm. Reverend James and all of the Jesuits were arch defenders of Pope Paul VI's encyclical, Humanae Vitae.

Discussions regarding aspirations and the cultural make-up of the area were many. There were, within the territory of the high school, the well-to-do, the middleclass, and sons of families just scraping by. There were students from one-million-dollar homes, and others from wooden shacks. There was the majority who spoke only English, and several recent immigrants who still had difficulties with the English language.

Although we highly regarded our teacher, it wasn't really until we went to Martyrs' Shrine that we saw him in his true element. The grave and relics of St. Jean de Brebeuf meant so much with our high school being named after that illustrious saint. We prayed the Stations of the Cross together. Any questions we had, Reverend James answered before we could find a tour guide. It was while he was talking to several men from the Rama Nation, who were there on a retreat, that Reverend James appeared almost angelic.

The next day at the start of class he asked us one question, "Is it right to remove native children from their reserves?" The forty-three minutes of time allotted for any class was not enough for all of the comments. Although we didn't know it at the time, the issue was equally important to him in Winnipeg and had since never been dismissed.

There was no student that he ever let drift or whose question was not considered important. All were treated equally.

Unfortunately when our class graduated in June 1968, we were not empowered to grant sainthood to our gentlemanly teacher who meant so much to us.

Reverend James' career as a teacher lasted until he was sixty-five years old in 1981. After that he was assigned to a parish north of Toronto. That position lasted only three years.

Thereafter he was transferred almost 3,000 kilometers to the east, to St. Pius X Parish in St. John's, Newfoundland.

This must have been a shock to his system. First of all, Reverend James was being so far removed from the love of his life: teaching Grade Nine students. Then he was being placed in a spiritual environment that had in years past been relatively stagnant. That disposition did not in any way reflect a unique attitude in that parish. In fact, the St. Pius X community was extremely receptive to everyone attending and to varying ideas and differences. Always having a welcoming mind meant so much. However, there remained that element in society in general that wished to maintain the status quo.

The Jesuit Order had first established a parish in Newfoundland more than three hundred and fifty years before in 1627. Political turmoil involving wars between the French and English interfered with the spiritual aims of both the Catholic and Anglican communities. The Jesuits had to leave, and ultimately returned in 1784.

The Catholic Church in Newfoundland under the direction of Archbishop Roche experienced spiritual stability during the years of his episcopate from 1915 to 1950. However, this prelate was a staunch conservative and became one of the leaders opposed to Confederation. His successor too was opposed to significant rapid change. Archbishop Patrick Skinner did not actively support many of the changes proposed by Vatican II Council. He in fact had voted for them, but implementation was not quick or thorough. Archbishop Penny in 1980 wanted to change all that by directing the Church in Newfoundland to fully embrace the Post-Vatican II era.

For six years until 1990, Reverend James' efforts, liturgical mission, and his instruction were all well received. Parish groups discovered a new inspiration. Children in parochial schools found a friend ready to participate in recess-time sports. Homilies stressing the rebirth of Catholic practice received attentive response. Benediction in accord with his liturgical agenda became a regular devotion. Above all else in those few years, Reverend James reached out to those who felt disenfranchised by the Church and society.

At the time of his arrival in 1984, the urban population was approximately 160,000. That figure included the residents in twelve surrounding communities. St. John's citizens formed approximately thirty percent of the entire island.

The aboriginal population within the city was less than six percent of that figure, being indigenous persons espousing Cree, Métis, and Mi'kmaq heritage. The Cree were distant relations of the Montagnais from Quebec. With the Métis, Reverend James was well-acquainted from his many years in Manitoba. Both the Cree and Métis were conversant in French. That provided access to spirited communication enabling him to support and encourage those indigenous persons.

However, it was the last group that provided most of Reverend James's interaction with the aboriginal community. The Mi'kmaq (commonly referred to as 'Micmac') encompassed many tribes and communities under many names with varying languages and dialects. They were not one homogenous group. Rather their territories occupied regions within every province and state of Eastern North America. The Mi'kmaq were also referred to as Abenaki, Gaspesian Tribe, Porcupine Indians, Restigouche, Kespu'kwitk, Piwktuk, Unama'kik, Shonack, Souriquois, Cape Sable Natives, Passamaquoddy, Tarateen and Taqamkuk. Their language was closely related to the Algonquian tongue. However, dialects were significantly different, making communication at times between communities quite impossible.

The Mi'kmaqs in Newfoundland experienced a whirlwind of disappointments. Recurring epidemics and white man's typhus had decimated their populations. Those diseases had already exterminated the Beothuk Nation. The choice very early to fight with the French against the English repeatedly caused much tribulation throughout the indigenous nation. Immigrants from Europe became a pestilence decimating the inherent industries and life style of the Mi'kmaq communities. Railroads invaded their territory, removing trees and logs, while mills and industry destroyed streams and polluted rivers.

The Christian Church too had its pathetic impact forcing a spiritual creed upon a people who already embraced beliefs that encompassed all of nature. Not only people, but animals, the sun, flowing rivers, trees and even rocks possessed a spirit that was eternal. There was no distinction between natural or spiritual or supernatural. They had their creation story and their belief in supernatural beings that took the form of animals to guide each person in their quest. The extended family was the basic unit within a tribe. Each community had a chief and the leaders would meet at least once every year. Shamans were available for every person to interpret and guide.

It was this culture that Reverent James understood. His acquaintance with indigenous beliefs and aspirations had prepared him for this mission. There were only a few within the parish who professed to be Mi'kmaq, and who similarly found their beliefs in nature and all creatures to be so soothing.

One wonders if Reverend James, while he was in St. John's, was also asked the questioned posed to him in our Grade Nine Class more than twenty years before: "Is there a place for animals in heaven?" Witnessing the blind person who relies on the guidance of a dog, hearing about a woman being awakened by her cat to escape a house fire, or viewing the work of police-dogs, these realities always prompt such concepts when Christ tells us that in heaven, "There are many mansions." So much comfort and hope could be found in the Mi'kmaq reverence of nature.

Reverend James then extended his agenda to securing land and equipment for playgrounds and promoted the construction of retirement homes. If he could do more to help them, he did. Reverend James was endeared to these native persons in Newfoundland as much as he was to the indigenous people and to everyone in need whom he met throughout his ministry.

Illness returned in 1991, in his 75TH year, to the extent he could no longer function. After being transferred to the infirmary in Pickering, Reverend James Toppings entered eternity on March 2, 1991.

The gospel reading on that Saturday in the 2ND week of Lent was the Prodigal Son. Like the father who embraced his long lost son, Reverend James had always been there to welcome and provide guidance and comfort to so many who needed a kind word or reassuring smile.

He is well remembered.

1996

KEVIN

Dancing bears pranced across the screen. Excited with the possible result, the middle-aged man glued his eyes to the flashing images. There was every expectation that in just seconds the bells would once again ring, lighting up the monitor. The exclamation of "Jackpot!" had to happen. It could be in a second, the next minute, perhaps even an hour; or never. Kevin pressed the button once more. It was an automatic impulse that had become the logical norm.

To his left, an old woman slowly pushed her spin-button, seemingly lacking any urgency for the 'big win'. Kevin cursed the stupidity of such quarter bets. "What's she to gain? A couple of bucks?" That would never be enough to satisfy his whim. Actually it was much more than that. His was an absolute compulsion. However, he was not then or ever about to realize the folly of his obsession.

"Krazee Koalas" was his favourite slot machine. The graphics were so extraordinary. "How could anyone design such graphics?" Such ingenuity always amazed him. "Can't we make these machines in Canada?" He deplored the idea that the provincial government was importing such machines from Australia. "Don't we have the research here?" A series of queries was quite the norm to prompt him to think 'outside the box'. "To restrict oneself to status quo is like jumping into the abyss." Kevin could dab in philosophy when it suited his interest.

Two hours was the norm, but on that Sunday evening he had long exceeded the standard. Another twenty-dollar bill slipped into the machine without a thought. The more he had in his pocket, the less he contemplated the amount. There always was an immeasurable flow of bills: too many to count and too few to cause worry.

That day was different from his regular routine. Normally he'd be jumping from machine to machine, but chose instead to remain steadfast to the stool in front of his favorite screen. He much disliked the term 'machines' because they were more his friends. They shared a strange companionship, and he attributed to them an instinctive recognition of his presence. Too often he had heard a strange calling, almost a congratulatory beckoning, the moment he pushed the sacred button. The jackpot bells would start ringing before the tumblers even completed their rotation.

The old woman cursed her slot machine and left in a huff. Instantly, another person sat down. She was obviously one that had taken the casino bus because she was constantly looking at her watch if not at his screen. Others in the row were so capti-vated by the animated activity flashing before them. There seemed to be this crazy perception that there was a direct corre-lation between the manner in which they stared at the machine or rubbed the monitor and the prospect of a sizeable payoff.

The terms 'payoff' and 'win' bothered Kevin to no end. If the spin generated a payout of $1.50, the casino called it a win. Kevin knew differently. If he bet a dollar to generate a win-fall of a $1.50, he really only won fifty cents. But then, the customers were not brilliant individuals and accepted whatever they put in their pocket at the end of the day as their winnings even though the amount was far less than that when they arrived.

There was a mystique about casinos that drew many, even those who couldn't afford it, to the slot machines. The bottom line was clear that more left angry than those who left smiling. Actually he had heard that the payout level was normally less than five percent. He had also heard two percent. Those casinos that guaranteed ten percent were therefore more in demand. Kevin analyzed the math: if everyone bet the same amount on each spin, and stayed the same length of time, then for every person who won nine would leave the casino as losers. And that was the best case scenario.

Accordingly he challenged the situation where the general manager of the casino operations was not an elected member of the provincial government. That didn't make sense based on Kevin's understanding of politics. This also proved that Kevin tended to be naive with respect to political matters and commentary as more often than not he believed everything he was ever told. He had no idea if all that was ever rumoured about the manager was the truth, but it sounded good.

Although he was mesmerized by "Krazee Koalas", Kevin constantly looked over his shoulders to view the machines behind him. The mixed-sevens and the blazing-sevens were sure to pay a jackpot shortly. There were three attendants in the area. They wouldn't be there unless one of them suspected there'd be a hand-paid jackpot. Casino life was like that. You couldn't follow the money, but you could always spy the attendants.

The old man to his right continued to annoy Kevin. It wasn't cigarette smoke or body odour. The old guy just continued to play thirty lines times one coin. The denomination was a penny. It bothered Kevin even more that the senior citizen would be pleased with any payoff even less than a dime.

Of course that would not have been an option before the slot machines started accepted bills and giving voucher slips. For years the player had to drop endless coins into a slot. That took time. Sixty dollars would easily last an hour. Now anyone could lose twenty dollars in a matter of minutes.

Kevin dutifully used his player's card. He never understood the reluctance of others to avoid it. Another person suggested the machines controlled who would get jackpots; as long as you had your player's card in the slot, the machine knew if you had already won enough that day, week or month. The one benefit of using the card for Kevin was the free meals and the monthly hotel that kept his family on board.

By the time he left the casino just after ten o'clock, Kevin had lost far more than he anticipated. There were only two bills left in his pocket. Everything he lost came from a credit card. He had five of them. Their use and even existence was discreet. The bills arrived at his business address.

Kevin was self-employed as an automobile damage appraiser. Although he advertised vehicle repairs, he was well known within the community for his expertise involving other means of transportation: boats, skidoos, trailers, snow-mobiles and motorcycles. His business was well known also for his generous support to so many charities. His promotion involved at least fifteen charity golf tournaments. At least twice every month he was taking adjusters to lunch. He never believed too much in treating senior management, as it was the junior staff who decided which appraiser was the most efficient and available for their needs.

The casino world was just his means of escape. He really didn't have to run from anything. Business was great and the family life was even better.

His spouse of fifteen years, Caren, was a very dear woman: always so diminutively enthusiastic. They had two children who were always well fed, excelled in school, and achieved significantly in sports.

Caren had supported his decision to abandon a seemingly solid position with an insurance company where he had been its senior appraiser. There was also a junior estimator with only three years experience. Then management decided to drop a few brokers. With the reduction in business there would be fewer claims. Having quality insured persons, who didn't get into accidents, meant substantially less work for the appraisers. With the differential in wages between the two employees doing the same job, he could very well be the one who was dispensable.

Choosing to become a self-employed appraiser opened the door to still do the appraisals for all insurance companies who were stuck with poor drivers. Acquaintances in the legal profession also used his services for appraisals under the statutory appraisal condition of the Insurance Act. Kevin's involvement in the dispute litigation process expanded his reputation significantly. He was at that time well regarded for his thoroughness and prompt reports.

It was in the litigation process that this author first met Kevin. The case involved a contractor's negligence that caused a fire damaging the stock and premises of several tenants.

Kevin had been involved identifying the actual cash value and replacement cost of the fineries and stock of one of the merchants. Success was the result, and most participants in the mediation were pleased with the outcome. Some of us were returning home to various cities by train which unfortunately required us to wait for another couple of hours. Rather than sit in the train station we adjourned along with the adjusters and appraisers to the local drinking establishment. After supper, the young ladies commenced their show displaying their presence. In the course of the second performance a young lady stood near our table with her back to us. A gentleman in our group made a lascivious comment about her attributes and asked her to turn toward us. Immediately an adjuster in our group fainted and fell on the floor gasping. The topless young lady was his daughter. It's hard to forget meeting people under those circumstances.

Conversations between Kevin and the author continued after that, on and off for the next few years.

There was little conversation upon his return home. The children were already in bed, fast asleep. They had talked excitedly all evening with their mother about the outing that was planned for the Monday. Kevin had no intention on that Easter Sunday, the seventh of April in 1996, that it would end this way. After eating early supper with his visiting sister-in-law he initially had not planned to spend the rest of that evening in a casino.

Caren was seated on the couch, already in her nightgown. She didn't say a word. Her anger was clearly intense. She wasn't irate about his loss, because in reality she had been fed lies for the past two years. Every time he went, he reported winning a lot or losing minimal amounts. He always put food on the table and was a great dad in terms of time and activities with the children. She had heard so many times from her limited number of friends about what other men were like. Kevin was an angel compared to these.

Her Ukrainian heritage taught her so many fundamentals of courtesy, dignity and sacrifice. Caren truly believed that she surrendered herself the moment she said, "I do." Her commitment was total no matter the cost. In moments of anger, she rarely raised her voice. Silence was the best method to ponder the circumstances. Her children were exceptional. Her husband's business was profitable. She should have been living the dream of a perfect family.

Conversation flowed across the breakfast table the next morning. Laying wide awake all night, he had committed himself once more to never again entering another casino. That eased all stress. He had identified the dilemma and vowed that he had fixed the problem.

Kevin's parents were Algonquian, being devoted to the heritage and culture that made them so fundamentally important within their native community. He held a tribal card, but that had for many years been buried among redundant paperwork. Algonquian was in his past. He might refer to it someday, sometime, but for now there was no need of it.

One of his clientele in a business conversation wildly suggested there were significant generic traits common to all natives. He somehow got to that conclusion after someone mentioned recent storm damage in a remote community. Kevin had to bite his lip and just listen. Alcohol, gambling and thievery were the common tendencies that person ascribed to each and every person within all of the indigenous communities. After that discussion Kevin tried earnestly to avoid that particular individual. Silence was perhaps better than allowing himself to vehemently reply to false insinuations. At the time, Kevin was still stricken by the news of his parents' death. The legacy of such tragedies never died. He spoke rarely of the event. Hearing white men talk so disdainfully about aboriginals brought to life his many questions, thoughts, and dread. He was the surviving member of his family, but he never chose it to be that way.

Kevin had met Caren in Winnipeg. They both belonged to the same Catholic community. Religion was one of the few aspects of life that gave him hope. They moved to Windsor one year after their marriage. Kevin, with appropriate training, then established his expertise as an appraiser. They purchased a house within the first year of the move. Months later, Caren's father was dead. Her mother passed away just two years after that. As neither Kevin nor Caren had surviving parents, they were very much the king and queen of their own realm. Everything so far had been a wonderful fairy tale.

Easter Monday was spent with the family visiting Story Book Gardens in London. Caren's sister joined them just to be with her nephews. Caren's sister was always a welcome guest to share pleasant times. It was as expected a wonderful day with lots of rides and adventure. The meandering river was as expected the main attraction on a warm sunny afternoon.

Kevin's week was always scheduled, with little deviation. During the spring, summer and fall months, there'd be a golf game on a Wednesday or Thursday. From noon time on Friday to Monday morning all hours were devoted to the family. That left him basically three days per week at his business. Realizing there was true value in life away from the office, he hired an office manager. Two secretaries completed the staff. The workers were well paid and the profits continued to fill the safe.

In autumn of 1996 he expanded the business, focussing on being a major parts supplier for foreign vehicles. That business prospered with so many car owners wishing to hold onto their present vehicles. That meant parts were essential, and he fulfilled that need.

Weekdays were not wholly committed to work. There always had to be time for the casino. Late nights, at least twice per week were the norm. Caren never said anything. If she was mad, silence would be her response. The truth could always be disguised with erroneous information regarding the result of his gambling. That was more often than not the reality.

The world and economics of the 1990s was not conducive to being thrifty and vigilant. The term 'honesty' had been replaced with everyone's propensity to use the ambiguous term 'transparency'. So it was for many lives, affecting many decisions, causing much folly. As long as it seemed to be the truth, then it was good for politicians, and unfortunately for families.

The computer world was causing havoc. Personal users and businesses jumped on board or they were quickly left behind. Kevin was astute enough to purchase the most current apparatus even if it meant having to replace equipment at least every year. Kevin felt very prepared for any unfortunate business situation. He had ever increasing profits, and repeatedly told himself, "a wonderful supportive family."

The demise did not happen radically. It was an ongoing situation that had started years before. With the increased use of computers many businesses and industries were concerned about checks and balances. The one that most affected Kevin was the decision of the insurance industry that any appraiser had to avoid participating in any salvage or parts firm. Clearly the insurance companies wanted to avoid a situation where an appraiser was falsifying a total loss assessment for his own personal gain. For Kevin, that had never happened. However, someone in the provincial capital thought it could.

He sold the parts business before the end of the year, yet discreetly remained involved. He had a win-fall of cash, with no specific plan for its use. Splitting the proceeds would be a benefit, so he allowed Caren to assume half of the profit.

It was just weeks before Christmas that Kevin, perhaps for the first time, identified his plight. Seven credit cards in excess of ten thousand dollars each were all maxed. His line of credit was gone. Not being able to speak with the banks over the Yuletide holiday caused significant consternation. He was clearly not happy throughout the holiday season.

1996 ended with sudden worries. He pledged to address those as soon as possible. Meanwhile he started cursing past decisions. Throughout that entire year, his casino losses surpassed his annual income. Strangely, he started thinking of his Algonquian heritage as if he was searching for a scapegoat.

One of the banks started his spiral into the abyss. Somehow, two of the credit card companies had, as their guarantee, the mortgage on his house. After missing minimum payments for several months, the amount owing on five cards was ascribed as a mortgage on the house.

Fortunately, he was able to make the mortgage payment every month, but with some difficulty. However, it required him to acquire another line of credit. He was losing ground fast. In those weeks and months he cursed his native heritage, clearly blaming his aboriginal ancestry for his gambling compulsion.

Kevin then struggled for months, barely succeeding. Caren remained happy, for she knew nothing of the circumstances. Her ignorance was inversely proportional to the pills Kevin required to function daily.

Profits continued their slithery slide down the frosty incline. As the insurance industry approached the millennium, the concern about expenses more than doubled. Drive-In Appraisal services were being established in every major city to control the cost of auto repairs. Preferred shops limited the involvement of independent appraisal firms. Cost controls hit every aspect of the industry.

Then Free Trade entered the picture. As soon as the federal government signed the NAFTA agreement, parts could be obtained cheaper elsewhere. The effect was devastating.

Caren discovered the mortgage situation with receipt of the semi-annual bank statement in mid 1997. Their vocal exchange echoed beyond the walls of their living room, making the children squirm with all of their imaginary fears. Kevin swore it must be a mistake and that he would attend the bank to correct the situation. Her anxiety was not abated. Something was clearly wrong.

Kevin experienced a radical monetary up-swing in the latter weeks of that year. The wintery weather and three blizzards were beneficial for business. At the same time, jackpots exceeding thirteen thousand dollars helped the situation. To ensure that Caren would no longer be bothered by any bank statement, he had those directed to a mailbox at the local post office.

With the spring of 1998, Kevin once again pledged to himself to change his ways and avoid the casino. Regardless of his good intentions he failed to fill the void in time with something constructive. Caren suggested he become an assistant coach for their older son's soccer team. That was their boy's favourite sport. He seemed all gung-ho, but Kevin's commitment never existed. Anger again brewed between husband and wife.

Kevin's ability to fight temptation remained pathetic. On one trip to inspect a damaged vehicle, he travelled past the casino. His car then automatically turned into the parking lot. His gambling loss was substantial. Equally so, he failed to make it to the scheduled appointment and lost that client's business.

At no time did he ever contemplate God's potential involvement in the cause, control or resolution of his gambling problem. After their move to Windsor, attendance at religious services was less than it had been, but they still believed. At the same time, Kevin perceived a world where he was in total control. This meant dismissing his heritage, and believing that nothing in his past determined his fate. He clearly did not have a specific goal or workable means. That was proving to be havoc. The one philosophical-biblical passage that could have helped him, he didn't even bother to consider.

> When an evil spirit leaves a person, it travels over dry lands looking for a place to rest. When it can't find one, it says to itself, "I will return." So it goes back and finds the entire house swept clean. Then it invites seven other spirits even worse than itself. They all entered and lived there; so that the person became worse than he was in the beginning. (Luke 11:24)

"Religion is for wimps," he had said on several occasions, even though he may not have meant it. The one inspirational means that could have saved him was abandoned. Similarly, he had no intention to ever surrender himself to the any 'Gamblers Anonymous' organization. After all, he wasn't about to publicly admit he had a problem. As long as he could hide the consequences, there was no problem.

Just before the summer of 1998, the author met again with Kevin. It was quite by accident. Under those circumstances, conversations generally are more likely to ensue. Even though the gambler had willingly admitted a problem to myself, he would not pursue the recommended treatment. It was discovered later that Kevin had similar discussions with other associates, and on each occasion rejected the recommendation for counselling. It may have been that he was just searching for anyone that would support him—perhaps telling him that he didn't have a problem. He had chosen to be his own doctor and patient, and was failing pathetically in both roles.

Anxiety passed with the family trip to Florida that summer. Although it was hot, it was a most delightful time. Epcot and Walt Disney World were of course the main attractions. Driving both ways didn't bother him. Kevin and Caren had a propensity for exploring small towns and enjoying the culture offered by the Atlantic states. That ensured that every family trip had wonderful memories.

After Labour Day, Kevin returned to hell. He had to win big in order to recoup his losses. Accordingly, incidents at the casino became even more damning. He'd leave a machine, and minutes later it would pay a jackpot. If he had a choice of two machines, he'd choose the wrong one. He was never one for poker. Kevin tried blackjack and the losses were monumental. He played craps, and similarly the loss was immeasurable. Four credit cards, each with more than ten thousand maximum limit, were acquired based on his lies to the financial companies. That was quite easy. He went to four sporting events, and left with a t-shirt on each occasion after filling out a credit card application. He was always borrowing from one card to make the minimum payment on another. As long as no one called, the bills were concealed and minimum payments made everything copacetic.

The amorous life between Kevin and Caren remained active. They had pledged to have no more children and accordingly took the appropriate precautions.

Caren's sister, called the author out of the blue just before Thanksgiving in 1998. Surprise hastily became an ear for a worried soul. The woman had too many suspicions. These were instigated by Caren's talk of Kevin's late nights, and affirmed when a mutual friend observed Kevin at the slots when he should have been at work. Every aspect of the family's life was divulged. The woman's tone conveyed she was firm in her beliefs. "I don't want my sister hurt," she concluded. The author pledged to do what he could to address the situation, particularly speaking once again with Kevin.

It was in the last week of October, that the depths of Kevin's depravity consumed any hope for resolution. While at the casino, he enviously eyed a young man who had his arms around two blonde girls. He acted like a pimp. He was known to be a pimp. The young man bet $100 chips on numbers 4, 7 and 29 on each of ten roulette tables. Kevin quickly did the math. That was $3,000.

There were immediate shouts of surprise and joys when the ten roulette wheels stopped. The young man had won on seven of the tables. The total win was $24,500; actually $21,500 considering he had bet $3,000.

Kevin and others, whom he did not know, celebrated with the young man. Before the pimp returned to Detroit, the hospitality suite was offered to those who joined the festivities. There, Kevin was serviced by one of the ladies. When the author had heard this story and Kevin's willing voyage into decadence, he was absolutely shocked. Although he had never met Caren, he immediately felt sorry for any woman or any family who was so disgraced by the husband's illicit activities.

At the same time, Kevin had only three insurance companies still supporting his business. All others had abandoned him because he just didn't keep appointments. The quality of his assignments was constantly being questioned. He only kept the three clients because the managers there were also enticed by slot machines or frequented drinking establishments till almost midnight.

In the second week of November in 1998, the author was released from his position with the insurance firm for whom he had worked for twenty-three years. Any contact directly with Kevin died after that.

Kevin's choices were three: a weapon, a rope or pills. His sister-in-law described the events after the final incident. He had gone as far as to cross the American border to purchase a gun. Kevin attended his family doctor for medication for depression and reproduced the prescription to acquire more depressants than he could have ever logically used. He already had the rope in the garage. However, any prospect of any such foul deed quickly dissipated.

He won two jackpots, enough to cover the mortgage payment and credit card demands. That assured him money for Christmas gifts. ·

Then, in the second week of December, he was offered a job with a lucrative salary. The position would require the family to move. Caren absolutely refused and told him he'd have to go by himself.

He couldn't afford his debts on his present income. The bank had never said 'no' to increasing his line of credit such that now his gambling debt was more than seventy percent of the value of their house.

Kevin's sister-in-law met with the author in the third week of December. She shed tears of anger and frustration. The cause of her gloom was readily discernible. She advised that she had spoken with Kevin and was shocked at the degree of preparedness to end his life. That he had even mentioned these aspects shocked her no end. Kevin dismissed her sympathy and offer of financial support with the pathetic opinion that all of his problems were due to his parent's heritage. She had also offered to call the family doctor regarding his unstable situation. Kevin swore refusing her assistance. In spite of that, she pledged to call the doctor the next morning.

There was no need for a call to the family doctor. There were no presents under the Christmas tree. The coroner attended as required. Kevin had determined his fate. The empty pill bottles affirmed the cause.

Meanwhile, the provincial income from its casino operations that year exceeded one billion dollars.

1999
Bishop Lawrence Sabatini

Among the squalor of impoverished immigrants, the Sabatini family welcomed their fourth child. Born on May 15, 1930, Lawrence entered the world of people scrounging for daily sustenance. This was the Italian community of northwest Chicago. Its only saving grace was the fact that it wasn't buried downtown amidst racial turmoil and the criminal element. Yet, their enclave was not substantially different from any other urban centre in America. The rich got wealthier while the residents of tenement buildings languished without fundamental expectations. The division between the poor and the opulent had become an outrageous chasm that was never to be transgressed. If born poor, you stayed poor. All of the rhetoric about American opportunities and equality: all those promises had bypassed more than ninety percent of the population. Jobs were scarce, and wages pathetic. Landlords gouged, and families starved.

Their parish church, Our Lady of Sorrows, was unfortunately most aptly named. Three years after his birth, his family, the entire neighbourhood, all of North America and the entire world were thrown into society's cesspool—the Great Depression. Lawrence's father struggled as did everyone else: losing employment and then begging for jobs. If employment could be arranged, no one with any sense was brazen enough to expect a reasonable salary.

Lawrence's father was lucky. Chicago had been the hub for so many rail lines that were still engaged in rapid expansion into the west. It was the railroads that kept produce moving, as well as becoming the home for so many who had lost everything. Pullman, Illinois, a suburb in south Chicago, provided that opportunity for work. He knew when he grabbed the job that it might be months or perhaps even years before he would see his family again. Any salary he earned could be dispatched by the same railway company back to his family. So many Italian journeymen joined the ranks laying track as far west as Nevada and the Rocky Mountains. Our Lady of Sorrows was smiling.

As soon as the recession ended, the talk of war began. Although America had fought the request to join the Allies, there was no option after Pearl Harbour. His father went to war, and fought bravely for our freedoms.

Lawrence was in Grade Five when America committed its troops to the war effort. He was a devout altar boy appreciating how religious liturgy inspired his timid soul. Timid he was, as naturally he would be. No child at that time could count on anything to ever be consistent in his/her life. In a moment's whim everything could instantly change.

His desire to be a priest came early and stayed throughout the rest of grade school and into high school. Sports were also his delight, especially baseball and pitching. Lawrence developed a unique tendency for a child his age, which he further enhanced during his teens, to throw various pitches that constantly baffled batters. He saw sports as a relief from the uncertainty of daily activities even though his Chicago Cubs failed four times that decade to win the World Series. Although he never made it to the professional or semi-pro ranks, one of his friends mastered a pitch Lawrence taught him. It was the 'screw ball', wherein the wrist is flipped outwards. The ball approaches the batter about chest high and then suddenly drops to his knees on reaching home plate. Major League baseball was that friend's ultimate destination.

Once he completed high school, Lawrence was determined to enter the seminary. He had so impressed his pastor by his devotion and academic ability that he found himself destined for Italy to attend the Scalabrini Seminary in Rome. The Fathers of St. Charles, the Scalabrini Fathers, had administered his parish and guided him in his vocational pursuit. That religious order had been established in 1887 by Bishop Giovanni Scalabrini of Piacenza, Italy. The intent of the order was to administer to the spiritual needs of Italian immigrants with a special focus on those immigrating to America at the start of the century. Bishop Scalabrini had even engaged President Theodore Roosevelt in discussions regarding the implementation of social programs. Their influence then expanded to not only consider the needs of the Italian community but also other immigrants, to the extent they were established in more than twenty countries.

Following the completion of courses in philosophy, theology and canon law, Lawrence was ordained on the Feast of St. Joseph, March 19 of 1957. A short span of parish work preceded his assignment to teach seminarians at St. Charles Seminary in Staten Island, New York. Canon Law was his specialty. He was also very proficient in church history and the classics. Saints Anselm, Augustine, Thomas More and his namesake Lawrence were the focus of his interest. His mind was incredible being able to remember pertinent details of so many issues. At the same time he kept active with sports, preferring baseball above all else while enjoying the opportunity to swim in the massive block-reinforced outdoor pool. The liturgy still had a special place in his spiritual life. Accordingly, he looked forward to the implementation of the changes proposed by Vatican II Council. Getting the laity more involved was a fundamental goal.

While stationed at the seminary, Reverend Lawrence expanded his efforts to include the poor, hungry and homeless in the port area of Staten Island and in mid-Manhattan. There were always more than enough people requiring assistance to keep him busy. At the same time, Reverend Lawrence was improving his colloquial skills in additional languages. The work among the poor in New York brought him face to face with members of the Latino communities. Being conversant in both Spanish and Portuguese was essential to adequately listen and attend to their needs. He had already developed proficiency in French, so with his knowledge of Latin, he had the amazing ability to converse in five languages. He pledged that German was to be his next.

The author met Reverend Lawrence in the summer of 1966 at our parish church in Toronto. Our associate-pastor had been involved in a serious motor vehicle accident three years before and never fully recovered. With our parish expanding so quickly, another priest was definitely required. That summer, Reverend Lawrence was that cleric.

His love for baseball was easy to see. The parish had a massive field behind the church which was levelled for the use of summer league baseball. The smiles and enthusiasm were incredible as boys and girls who had never participated in organized sports were suddenly hitting the baseball to the perimeters of the park. That was the 'heyday' for the youth of our parish. Reverend Lawrence was the key ingredient that made it all happen.

His interest in church history attracted both men and women in their respective parish groups. He'd always start with a puzzling question that engaged many with personal opinions. After that, he would summarize the church's teaching. Reverend Lawrence, on several occasions, visited St. Augustine's Seminary in Toronto, most likely to discuss curriculum. Afternoon discussions involved our Auxiliary Bishop in the parish near ours. He took the altar boys to see a Toronto Maple Leafs Baseball game. Reverend Lawrence spent many hours talking with the workmen at various projects. Sunday afternoons found him at the Italian soccer club. Liturgical devotions remained his focus, being available to address the spiritual needs of the parishioners. On the First of September, he left for New York.

While we were focussed on efforts in Eastern Canada, the Scalabrini Fathers were busy considering the needs of the immigrants in Western Canada. Following the war, there was a massive influx of Europeans into all regions of the Dominion. Principal among these were the Italians. The Provincial Superior for the Order accordingly left Winnipeg to explore possible venues for his first parish in the west. That church he established in New Westminster. Reverend Lawrence became part of the overall plan of expansion and in 1971 was transferred 4,800 kilometers to the west to Vancouver, British Columbia.

Reverend Lawrence served there as a parish priest for seven years. We learned later that there were four elements that prompted his assignment: leadership ability, work with the impoverished, knowledge of canon law, and his ability to grasp new languages.

By the time Reverend Lawrence had arrived in British Columbia, residential schools were already the means of providing destitute native children with public education. Tragically, the children were abused to such an extent that they were permanently affected. The schools were established by the Anglican Church, the United Church, and the Oblate Missionaries for the Catholic religion. Father Lawrence questioned the need for such schools and the conditions within. Unfortunately, the recommendations of Trudeau's government that were announced in its 'White Paper' two years before were not fully implemented. The federal government did not take immediate steps to stop the abuse and charge the criminals. Meanwhile, the provincial government, that was just given the task, was not able to respond as quickly as common sense demanded it should.

Father Lawrence's interest was additionally focussed on the Italian-speaking adults. From St. Stephen's Church in North Vancouver he ministered to their needs, established the Catholic Women's League, arranged meetings for the Holy Name Society, and attended to the interests of the youth with CYO meetings, parish sports, Boy Scouts and Girl Guides. There were two parish choirs, and more than forty altar boys. Regretfully, the number of new vocations to the priesthood was declining, leaving all priests in the province hard-pressed to fulfil their daily spiritual agenda. That there were more than 150,000 immigrants in the metropolitan Vancouver area certainly meant that there was never going to be any quiet time.

Vancouver at the time of the cleric's arrival was home to the Coast Salish Nations, as well as being a refuge for some Métis and Inuit. Those belonging to the Salish Nations totalled approximately ten thousand. Among that number there were some who had adopted the Catholic faith to augment their way of life and support their love of God's grandeur. His linguistic abilities aided Reverend Lawrence in communicating with these residents. It is indeed most appalling that society concocted generalizations that prevented adequate housing, proper sustenance, basic health care and quality education. It wasn't just the residential schools that were abusing indigenous peoples. It was also the haphazard manner in which the needs of the native communities were being brushed aside.

Reverend Lawrence's efforts were noticed, and in 1978, specifically on July 15TH of that year, he was consecrated Auxiliary Bishop of Vancouver. This position provided the opportunity to have another priest appointed to St. Stephen's Church. Meanwhile, Bishop Sabatini's calendar became ever more congested with spiritual and social events throughout the diocese.

At the same time, respecting his influence and commitment, Lawrence was appointed by the Holy See as the Titular Bishop of Nasai in Algeria. He was never able to visit the territory, choosing instead to send Episcopal Letters through the parishes to the Catholics in the Arab state.

As soon as he was designated a bishop, Lawrence Sabatini became a member of the Canadian Conference of Catholic Bishops. In that assembly, Bishop Sabatini served on the Episcopal Commission for Canon Law, and on the Commission for Migration. Both of these appointments reflected his strengths.

As always, Bishop Sabatini was committed to the ideals and benefits of Catholic Education. British Columbia chose not to entrench the obligation to entirely fund separate schools when the province joined Confederation. That became a major obstruction to Catholic education. In spite of limited resources, the Sisters of St. Ann in the 1880s established the first Catholic schools in Victoria and Kamloops. Tuition had to be paid exclusively by the parents or the Church. Ultimately, the province amended the funding formula by enacting the Catholic Independent Schools program in which classes for the primary grades were funded, but there was no financial support for the purchase of land, the construction of buildings or high school classes.

After the passage of that legislation, some academic funding beyond grade eight was provided. However, the majority of the tuition still had to be paid by the parents or the Catholic parish.

The Catholic Church still had to buy the land and build its own schools.

Then, in 1957, the Vancouver Archdiocese established a non-profit society. As a result of that decision, the Catholic Public Schools of Vancouver Archdiocese could save funds by achieving tax reductions. The consequence was beneficial. Catholic schools within the Archdiocese increased in number and size such that there were more than thirty Catholic primary schools and eight Catholic secondary schools. This was the situation Bishop Sabatini inherited: Catholic schools filled to capacity with waiting lists. Parents partially funding education caused a significant strain on most family incomes. However, the Archdiocese within its schools had an academic population committed to improving spiritual wellbeing and the community in general with a strong foundation for the future. Maintaining those expectations was Bishop Sabatini's mandate.

Throughout his years as Auxiliary Bishop, he remained very mindful of the condition and plight of the Salish Nations and all indigenous persons within the Archdiocese. He genuinely supported all programs that improved their conditions. Essential services, in his view, were absolutely mandatory. However, there were the chiefs, the provincial government and the federal government who all professed to know better espousing plans that very much repeated the follies of the past.

In September, 1978 Auxiliary Bishop Sabatini was consecrated Bishop of Kamloops. In that capacity he automatically assumed an undefined role in urban social affairs. It was almost impossible to separate the church and state in certain functions as both were keenly involved in the planning and direction of community events in a city of approximately sixty thousand people. That figure included the population within many suburbs.

Kamloops was first discovered by explorers in 1811. Native settlement had predated their arrival by at least four hundred years. In the 1860s the region was inundated during the gold rush.

The city is situated at the junction of two branches of the Thompson River near Kamloops Lake. It also forms the junction of the CNR and CP Railways. Kamloops is the interchange of highways heading east, west and north. The entire city could best be described as a hub of activity. Current industries include: Domtar Pulp Mill, Lafarge Cement, Highland Valley Copper Mine, Thompson Rivers University, Royal Inland Hospital, agriculture, the city itself and many businesses deriving their income from tourism.

When Bishop Sabatini arrived, the aboriginal population comprised approximately seven percent of the population. Accurate figures are not available as there was a native reserve right within city limits and not all of its residents were counted as being indigenous. With increasing pride in native culture, many who could claim kinship with the aboriginal community were returning to experience their heritage. The native population increased to nine percent of the city's population within ten years.

The indigenous people included those who could claim hereditary rights dating back to the initial natives who settled the region in the 15TH century. These were the Cree-Saulteaux, the Shuswap and the Interior Salish Tribes. Also within the city were groups of Métis from Manitoba, and Inuit who moved south from the Territories.

From Sacred Heart Cathedral, Bishop Sabatini began his mission devoted to creating an active laity. Unfortunately, not too many residents had any interest in his efforts. More than thirty-five percent of the city's population had no religious affiliation. If the indigenous population was included in that figure, it still meant that more than twenty-five percent of the 'white population' didn't care about God or religion. Roman Catholics were approximately seventeen percent, half of the number of Protestants. Hindu, Muslim, Jewish, Buddhist, Sikh and East Asian religions formed less than four percent of the population.

Bishop Sabatini's immediate steps included support for the Catholic Women's League, establishing Chaplaincy at the university, encouraging membership in the Knights of Columbus, supporting the Central Interior Fertility Centre, helping those experiencing marriage difficulties, and inviting the Franciscans and Carmelites to assist in the spiritual needs of the laity.

The Diocese of Kamloops, established in December, 1945, covers approximately 120,000 square kilometers. The borders today are the same as those when Bishop Sabatini assumed leadership. The diocese stretches from the Alberta border to the Strait of Georgia on the Pacific Coast. Whistler, Vernon and the Okanagan Valley are within territory. This diocese is one of five Roman Catholic dioceses in British Columbia. Kamloops, Nelson, Prince George and Victoria all report to the Archdiocese of Vancouver.

There were about 45,000 Catholics in the Diocese of Kamloops when Bishop Sabatini was assigned as its prelate. The clergy included approximately twenty-five priests, and a similar number of religious brothers and sisters. The diocese included forty-six churches in twenty-seven cities, towns or villages. Distances seemed to be forever doubled by the slow winding roads between mountains. No journey approached the speed limit. The weather was completely unpredictable. Snow and sleet could cover the roads when the rest of the province was basking in sunshine.

Bishop Sabatini's diocese ministered to the aboriginal communities. There were far more tribes within the entire diocese than in the city of Kamloops alone. In Williams Lake, the Sugar Cane and Soda Creek First Nations worshipped at Sacred Heart Church in that area. Fountain and Seton Portage First Nations worshipped at St. John the Baptist parish church in Lillooet. Natives of the Okanagan Reserve attended Mass at St. Theresa and St. Benedict churches in Vernon. St. Joseph on the Reserve Church was built for the Salish First Nation in Kamloops. In Merritt, the First Nations of Quilchena, Coldwater, Douglas Lake and Shulus were welcomed at Sacred Heart Chapel. The Mount Currie First Nation of Pemberton celebrated Mass at St. Francis of Assisi Church. Immaculate Heart of Mary Shrine in Cache Creek welcomed the Big Bear, Bonaparte and Deadman's Creek First Nations. The First Nation in Enderby worshipped at St. Mary's. In Barriere, members of the St. John Baptist First Nation worshipped at St. George's Church. There was also a parish church established for the Chilcotin and Shuswap Tribes of the Cariboo First Nation. In all, there were ten churches or chapels devoted to the spiritual needs of the First Nations. Liturgy included the sweet grass ceremony and expressions of peace not practiced in other parishes. Throughout his ministry, Bishop Sabatini expounded on the indigenous right to not only adequate but to equal health care, education, support for seniors and job opportunities.

After struggling and generating substantial success for seventeen years, Bishop Sabatini retired. After September 2, 1999, the prelate returned to his home in Chicago where he provided for the spiritual needs of a predominantly Latino parish.

Many may still remember his kindness and efforts. Not one Christian person or solitary member of the clergy stands alone as 'the Church'. "Together we form the Body of Christ on earth." It is that truth that drove Lawrence Sabatini to the nth degree to satisfy fervent aspirations and unlimited expectations.

His favourite prayer from the martyred Bishop Óscar Romero captured his personal perception of responsibility and achievement.

It helps us, now and then, to step back and take a long view. The Kingdom is not only beyond our efforts, it is even beyond our vision.

We accomplish in our lifetime only a tiny fraction of the magnificent enterprise that is God's work. Nothing we do is complete, which is a way of saying that the Kingdom always lies beyond us.

No statement says all that could be said. No prayer fully expresses our faith. No confession brings perfection. No pastoral visit brings wholeness. No program accomplishes the Church's mission. No set of goals and objectives includes everything. This is what we are about. We plant the seeds that one day will grow. We water seeds already planted, knowing that they hold future promise. We lay foundations that will need further development. We provide yeast that produces far beyond our capabilities. We cannot do everything, and there is a sense of liberation in realizing that. This enables us to do something, and to do it very well. It may be incomplete, but it is a beginning, a step along the way, an opportunity for the Lord's grace to enter and do the rest.

We may never see the end results, but that is the difference between the master builder and the worker.

We are workers, not master builders; ministers, not messiahs. We are prophets of a future not our own.

2003

GWEN

Life, no matter how much you venerate your Creator or nature, is not always coloured with bright floral displays, flowing wheat fields, meandering streams, majestic mountains and brilliant sunsets. There is also the vulgarity of needless death and blood spent upon the dust of county roads. We may well in life be preoccupied with all of the daily rituals demanding our time to which we respond by designating hours to specific tasks. But time is not ours to decide or to preserve; it is only ours for the giving.

> Not by a single moment can you
> alter life's span. (Luke 12)

The events in the paralegal's office were typical that morning. We can always assert we are overworked, but no one listens. Two trials in the following week demanded more attention than normal.

The call came to us just before 10AM on the morning of Tuesday, August 12, 2003. The voice I could not recall. He sounded very sincere as he asked for our assistance.

Geoffrey was a lawyer from a northern community who represented a First Nation in many of their legal matters. His forte was property and dispute resolution. In my work as a paralegal I always had the greatest respect for such individuals as they always put in ten to twelve hour workdays at least six days per week. They had to be 'geniuses' in almost all aspects of all litigation dealing with persons who were not conversant in the reasonable expectations of the white man's legal process.

He continued with his verse, making it almost near impossible to say 'no' to his ultimate request. Finally he stated it emotionally and simply as he could.

There was an accident. "Two are dead and the other driver is in hospital." That was devastating news. "The first nation may be involved." Clarification was requested.

After repeating that he had heard and read about our firm's expertise in civil litigation, he continued. This part of his description was a series of short phrases without a conclusion. There was a head-on collision. One driver seems to have been avoiding pot holes on the concession road. If he wasn't, there certainly were enough pot holes to prevent any vehicle from remaining on its own side of the road. Because there could be an allegation against the First Nation, Geoffrey felt he might be in a conflict of interest position.

His narrative continued. The driver who crossed the center line was alive and in hospital. He had been drinking before the accident according to the toxicology report at the hospital. There were no charges to that point in time. Geoffrey was rather firm on all of these issues.

Two adults in one car died at the scene. Their daughter, Gwen, is alive. Because he was asked to represent Gwen by an elder on the reserve, he felt he should obtain the best legal representative available to assist her. Responding to his faith, we took the case; and expressed our gratitude.

An hour later, a lawyer in our office called Geoffrey to verify the details. The accident occurred early on the Saturday morning, August 9TH. The rest of the information was confirmed. There was enough, but certainly much more was required.

An investigator was immediately retained to take scene photos and request the police report. Visiting the other driver, the one whom we would be suing, was primary. Getting his sworn statement before anyone else did would definitely be a major coup.

The next morning the adjuster reported by phone after being in touch with the police department. His advice was informative but very alarming.

The surviving child, Gwen, was only seven years old. She was a rear seat passenger in her parents' car. Her father was driving.

The police attended more than one hour after the accident. They were not called. The lone officer in his cruiser came upon the scene. The two adults in one car were clearly already dead. The morgue was called for them. An ambulance attended for Gwen. Another ambulance arrived for the other driver. The officer was acquainted with that driver because of several prior impaired charges.

The investigator's further advice painted a tragic picture. The responsible driver did not have insurance. After so many charges, more than likely, no firm would insure the unemployed individual.

All of the participants in the action were residents of the reserve. Gwen was an only child. There was no record of any aunts or uncles in that native community, although the officer was certain he could locate at least one in the adjacent reserve. One of the residents, a woman in her early forties, came to visit the child in the hospital. Gwen was there for two days and left in the accompaniment of that woman. The officer pledged to search for her name.

As to where the drunk driver had been indulging prior to the accident, the police had no idea and had not questioned him relative to any impairment as it seemed to the original officer on scene that the reason for crossing the centre line was the pot holes on the concession road.

Based on the minimal information available in that first week, a statement of claim was issued against that other driver for his negligence. The same document named the estate of Gwen's father as a defendant for his possible liability. Other litigation was commenced against the First Nation and the government relative to any negligence concerning the failure to maintain the road. At the same time, litigation was instituted against the Motor Vehicle Accident Claims Fund.

The entire venture started to resemble a very costly enterprise considering the limitations in our chance of success and the quantum we could realize. However, there was a child involved, whom none of us knew, who needed our help.

Both the police and the First Nation's Counsel could not tell us the name of the firm or person who graded the road smooth four days after the accident. That decision basically destroyed evidence. There were no scene photos immediately after the accident, so there could be no objective proof except that of the defendant driver who was not speaking. When the issue was pursued further, there was candidly no idea who could have or would have altered the terrain. Only the First Nation could benefit from such quick action in order to avoid any criticism.

It was presumed that the police force was an arm of the RCMP. About a week into the handling of the litigation, we realized that the officer and the force were operated by the First Nation. Matters, even involving serious charges, normally were handled by the provincial authority. Until the Criminal Code of Canada was violated, the RCMP would not be involved. The other driver still refused to provide a statement, almost as if he had the right to control and limit the investigation.

Proving the other driver's liability was going to be difficult unless he just folded. If we were able to affirm the impairment that would of course help our cause. However, the alcohol impairment tests were not taken within the statutory three hours for court admission.

The refusal of the driver to provide a statement hindered further enquiries relative to his lack of insurance. Was there any possibility of any coverage? Did he just fail to renew a policy? Was the policy improperly cancelled by an insurance company in mid-term? Was there any inappropriate action by an insurance broker? We did not know. However, he could not produce evidence of insurance and the police were satisfied he had none.

Similarly we were stymied in our attempts to obtain the name of the native resident or the firm where he was drinking excessively prior to the accident.

With his lack of automobile insurance, all venues were becoming bleak. We could not prove the First Nation's negligence for the lack of road maintenance, nor could we prove that the Chief or any member of the council ordered the subsequent re-grading. Proving any negligence by a host for the excessive alcohol was also extremely remote.

The cost of Gwen's treatment and rehabilitation was presented as an accident benefits claim on her father's policy. The claim for the funeral benefits and death benefits were also presented to the same insurance company.

The only venue for claiming general damages, with a maximum of $200,000 was against the Motor Vehicle Accident Claims Fund. The Fund responds only if there is no other valid insurance.

In typical fashion, the Fund fought our right to make the claim and confronted every step we took in the process. We were told that we had to prove that the other driver had no insurance. Once we crossed that hurdle, we had to prove he was totally responsible for the accident. If Gwen's father was just 1% negligent, then his liability policy would pay the entire claim and there would be no claim against the MVAC Fund for pain and suffering.

If Gwen's father was not at all liable, then the Fund had a right to deduct, from its potential payment of $200,000, all of the other benefits available to Gwen from all other sources. This became so much of a hypothetical situation as the First Nation provided support and care, the cost of some treatment, and incidental expenses such a daily assistance and transportation. Gwen and her legal representative had the right to claim either the costs of treatment from her father's insurance company or from the native community. However, the insurance company balked at granting approval if coverage with the reserve was available for the same treatment. The reserve generally would not keep records sufficient for litigation.

As a consequence, the first months of the entire claim were spent fighting the vulgar reality of systems that gave so little concern to the injured child. By Christmas of 2003, we vowed to change the passive attitudes of the government and the reserve. Gwen had to be everyone's primary interest.

The young child's injuries were considered 'serious'. The ambulance had transported her to a hospital off the reserve, and there she stayed for two tearful days. The impacts had forced the front seat back into the child, injuring her arms and legs. The back seat in which she was belted failed to remain structurally sound. Accordingly, she was forced into the back of the front seat as it was thrown towards her. That Gwen was alive was itself almost a miracle.

X-rays confirmed no fractures. However, there was significant facial bruising mainly across the forehead. Both wrists were inflamed. Her right knee caused excruciating pain. She couldn't straighten the leg. Once she was told that her parents died, the screams and tears were incessant.

Gwen had no family on which to rely. All homes on the reserve were several acres apart, so that the setting did not provide for familiarity among neighbours. The buildings were rented from the First Nation. What appeared to be mortgage payments were in reality rental fees. Very few were without running water. Electricity was a benefit for all. Most had septic tanks. In that the houses were significantly away from each other, prompted a sense of independence. That could be a benefit as long as one did not require a neighbour's assistance. The inescapable feeling of being all alone had driven stakes into her heart. She was old enough to realize the consequences of the tragedy.

There was only the one visitor, that woman approximately age forty. Thomas was her surname. She was a single mother with two children: ages thirteen and eleven. Her compassion reflected the common disposition towards others in need. The fact that she was the only one to visit conveyed the perception that the rest were too busy with their own needs.

Thomas provided a separate room for Gwen, a situation that her two children did not appreciate. They had little to call their own, and they were not ready to give up all that they had. Actually it wasn't much. Gwen's bedding was no more than an extra sheet. Gwen refused to eat the next morning, and insisted on only drinking warm liquids. Her dental issues had not been addressed. Mrs. Thomas raced to the Council Office that second afternoon with the child. A dental appointment was arranged. That required transportation to an office in the town as there was no dentist on the First Nation. Thomas also requested access to Gwen's house for her clothing. As a result, the back door was broken to gain access to the girl's wardrobe. Other goods that could be sold were taken to acquire funds to care for the girl's needs.

For treatment, most of it was provided by residents of the First Nation. The physiotherapy was not provided by a regulated physiotherapist, but rather by a woman acquainted with such techniques. Ice was the only treatment for Gwen's joints: up to four hours per day until the swelling decreased. Any psychological issues or neurological deficiency were addressed in one visit by a resident that the First Nation considered to be a specialist. None of this was wholly documented. Perhaps these persons were involved to keep costs payable by the community medical plan to a minimum; or perhaps they truly believed in their skills. So much of the provision of treatment was also very basic because of the limited funds from the federal government. Then of course there was the perpetual argument between federal and provincial departments on the provision of health care. Same is a provincial mandate, yet it is the federal government that provides funding for the operation of each reserve. That scenario did not help Gwen.

An occupational therapist was assigned by the law firm. Funding was not an issue as the office was willing to absorb the cost if the insurer balked at payment. Someone had to be involved to assist the girl and prepare an objective and detailed report. The paperless world was not helping Gwen.

The occupational therapist called our office three days after her assignment. Although she had called the Thomas family immediately, there was no cooperation. It was true Gwen had to attend school or the family had to do shopping, but the perception was quickly discernible that Thomas would not make the girl available for any appointment. Was she protective or defensive? Either argument could have been made. An idea in our office became a plan, and then a reality for me to visit the injured girl and her parental guardian, under the guise that we needed Thomas's signed consent forms.

Three days were planned and the motel accommodations were arranged. The occupational therapist struck me as a person most keenly interested in the patient. In the larger cities, the competition for business always seemed to create the perception that business interests preceded those of the injured persons.

Though this all sounds somewhat terse, the reality of the industry involved in the provision of care is such that the injured person is not always to all persons the primary concern.

Geoffrey's suggestion to us, that the condition of the Thomas residence was better than most, prepared me to believe that Gwen was fortunate to have such amenities. Whatever thoughts I may have had before our vehicle pulled into the driveway were immediately dispelled upon viewing the premises. Information twisted my mind even further. "How can this be?" The question demanding a reply echoed in my mind throughout the visit.

The house was a wood structure with some aluminum siding around the back, on one side, and on the lower portion of the front wall. The single pane windows were wood frame. The shingles were starting to curl. There was no eavestrough. The driveway was not smooth, basically gravel covering a culvert and winding from the side of the house to some unseen venue in the rear.

Thomas was clearly not ready for our visit as we came unannounced. Her attire conveyed a nonchalant attitude toward life. That was a quick conclusion. She was reluctant to open the door at first. I quickly addressed the need to have the forms signed. She hesitated, telling us she wanted to confer with tribal council. We stressed our need and ten minutes later she started to sign the documents on behalf of Gwen. Writing, even just her signature, was not her forte.

After she offered us coffee, she encountered difficulty remembering where she put the instant coffee. Similarly, it took time to find the powdered milk. I was not looking forward to the beverage.

Once the forms were signed, Mrs. Thomas became most talkative providing ample details of Gwen's initial injuries, her treatment, and present restrictions. She talked mainly in terms of the limitations rather than Gwen's abilities or daily activities. Such verse always prompted me to think that repeating details of injuries and limitations was an attempt to concentrate on a personal agenda. Did Thomas think she was going to get rich from this accident?

The need to go to the washroom was an automatic response to the coffee. Shock was absolute! She had described running water. The toilet was a commode over a hole in the plywood floor. There was no seat, and it was not connected to any plumbing system. It stunk as any outhouse would, perhaps less in winter than in mid-summer.

It was pointed out to me that there were also bathroom facilities in a wooden outhouse. This was on an incline behind the house. Between the structures a small two-foot wide stream flowed from the hill to the ditch at the start of the driveway.

The curtain in Gwen's bedroom was a blanket nailed to the wall. The occupational therapist looked inside the one drawer provided for Gwen, viewing the girl's personal clothes.

Later she described them as basic rags. We were told with a sense of pride that the community was assisting Mr. Thomas and helping Gwen. Eventually she responded to my queries by advising that "They're good people."

Questions about the family residence produced nothing positive. We were told that some items were removed as they could be used by others in the First Nation. We sensed that was her opinion on the inevitability of sharing.

After her son arrived, she asked him to get some water for supper. He picked up a tin pail. It did not appear to be overly clean. Thomas had running water in the kitchen; but for whatever reason, water from the stream was preferred. I watched as he went outside and filled the bucket from the same stream that was down the slope from the outhouse. That was enough for me.

Geoffrey was not available the next day, and the occupational therapist turned her attention to other clients. In the afternoon I returned, again unannounced, to the Thomas residence. It took time but eventually she understood the full purpose of our involvement and the reasonable expectations thereof. After the children returned from school, the offer was gladly received for supper in the mall. That it was about seventeen miles away provided another opportunity for discussion and acquaintance. The trust and faith of the children far exceeded that of their mother. In the course of the late afternoon and evening it was becoming very difficult to control my emotions. "Garbage makes them happy!" Though very crude, my mind could not escape the thought. "How can that be so? Has the press been lying to us? Why?" The last phrase constantly repeated itself while I tried as best as possible to appreciate their smiles. The most mundane events brought such joy to those children. It was equally impossible to escape the conclusion that our governments had been lying to us all these years about conditions and expectations, about their health care and education. "There but for the grace of God . . ." I concluded my prayer that night, thankful that there was at least an opportunity to assist.

If there was any one particular incident or issue that angered me most, it was not the bucket of polluted water, the lack of basic clothing, the lack of washroom plumbing, the lack of reasonable health care, the broken down school bus, the school portable with holes and rats or the lack of nutritious food—these were all important—but Gwen's wandering left eye.

There was definitely a neurological injury affecting her vision. There were facial injuries beyond the bruising that was first identified.

The discussion with Geoffrey was promising to shed more light on the situation with the hope that he could suggest medical experts that might not dismiss the injuries and impairment. As was the case in other sectors of society, such professionals would of course want to have the guarantee of prompt payment. Our own finances were limited. Any budget we had considered was already expended. The insurance company would have to be totally on board. There rested a major hurdle. Everything had been done through the First Nation and its medical benefits, such that the auto insurer had paid almost nothing in those first five months. To suddenly suggest that the child had a brain injury or vision problems or was catastrophically impaired in February 2004 would be confronting a brick wall. That meeting with Geoffrey ended after research and his recommendation for a case manager. She was a respected occupational therapist who was known to have, in the past, done work for that insurance company. The firm would be hard pressed to suddenly deny her expertise.

That assignment and the meeting with the case manager took place the next afternoon. Authorization forms were also provided. Thereafter I completed the five-hour return trip to the office.

Denials of treatment recommendations were inevitable. So much was in dispute and the insurance company was determined to go to mediation. In spite of the automobile insurer's arrogance, the service providers continued with treatment fully aware they would not received immediate payment.

Gwen's visions problems did not entirely resolve. However, she had continuing care and appropriate glasses. School marks and enthusiasm for life also improved. Her fears remained a stumbling block. Automobile transportation was so essential to get anywhere on the reserve or to leave the native community. All of her fears inside a vehicle were never totally vanquished. She remained timid, and at times very tearful. The passage of time did heal some of the emotional wounds. She rapidly matured after that first year. Everything she had experienced and all of her treatment provided emotional and spiritual parameters that proved to be of substantial benefit. She was taught to let go of the past as much as she could, and took that counsel seriously.

The case manager's report, after that first meeting stung the insurance company. Major renovations were recommended for the Thomas house for plumbing, heating and insulation. When those were rejected, efforts were made in conjunction with the interests of the Council to have Mrs. Thomas and her children move into Gwen's prior residence. Although the house had already been rented to others, adequate arrangements were made to have the house released to Thomas. Still, the litigation continued to assert the young lady's right to the cost of the renovations.

We expended great effort with statistics concerning employment and expectations. Both parents had been gainfully employed. The figures showed that such a foundation generally prompted children to pursue similar employment expectations. That claim was very significant.

Perhaps government officials were embarrassed by conditions on that reserve pertinent to health, education, plumbing and basic living. Schools received the initial funding. Portables were replaced by a brick extension to the main school building. School buses no longer broke down. Other buses would take patients to medical clinics on and off the reserve. Other improvements started to happen, albeit three years later, granting those residents a better way of life.

In 2010, the settlement mediation took place. Gwen looked almost angelic with her cultured style, mature appearance, bright floral dress, and black hair. She wore a green feather in her hair— a gift from her pet, reminding everyone of her parents' love of nature. The favourable result guaranteed the young lady and her guardian sufficient funds in a structured settlement to provide treatment, care and support well into the future. Gwen's parents were remembered with a monument at their cemetery.

For the sake of the child's privacy and to protect the integrity of the First Nation, it is again reminded that names have been altered to respect those involved.

Gwen's plight ultimately brought so many improvements to so many aspects of her life and fundamental conditions in the community. Her struggle will be remembered while her success in life brightens the morning sunrise.

LORIEN

"Non-descript" he preferred to call himself and accordingly chose to sit alone. Even though the assembly of more than several hundred lawyers occupied rows and tables around him, they couldn't encroach upon his domain.

His facial expression was attentive. The tuft on his chin suggested his age in the mid-thirties. His dark plaid suit conveyed a serious intent. His binder was open before him with several pens and his reliable note pad to the side. His satchel he had placed conveniently under the table. When others rose during the break to replenish their coffee, he just sat waiting for the next speaker.

This was the third time Lorien attended the Trial Lawyers' Conference. On prior occasions he too sat by himself. It wasn't in any way an attempt to avoid interruptions. He was there to learn from the expertise being shared by his colleagues. He valued the speakers' knowledge as all of the other lawyers claimed they did. However, he was far more earnest than most in that regard.

Lorien's office was more than four hours north of the city. Attending such a convention demanded his utmost commitment. Being a sole lawyer in a small office, with a clientele that could in a moment's notice potentially exceed several thousand, provided little time for personal convenience. Family life was once considered but never finalized.

He had already noted that many paralegals were in attendance. "If only I could afford one," he surmised. Lorien's clients were not all able to pay his services. The Legal Aid Program provided pittance for which a lawyer had to wait an eternity. He felt that was most unfair as the entire program seemed to hinder those who needed the assistance the most.

Lorien did not have a particular expertise. He was involved in property transactions and matrimonial disputes far more than civil litigation. Still, he knew one day that any knowledge he took from this convention would assist his practice.

I attended these conferences previously, always staying close to the select few from our office. The fact that our firm expected its employees to stay together throughout such events seemed to defeat one of the purposes of the convention. Rather than meeting new people, or being introduced to other lawyers; the company wanted to convey a level of unity among its ranks—even though most of the employees wanted to get away from their coworkers. This was the first time I saw the solitary gentleman. His profile suggested he was a distinguished gentleman. Having chosen not to have a third cup of coffee, I wandered over to his table to introduce myself. There was no smile, just an earnest expression.

After the initial exchange, Lorien controlled the conversation, asking more questions following each reply. That I was only a paralegal intrigued him most in terms of my tasks and authority. Clearly he was looking for assistance in his office. When he mentioned the location of his practice, my surprise was immediate. I always had difficulty hiding my feelings. When the next speaker took the podium, I returned to my group of coworkers where they were still patting each other on their backs.

For supper, our office got together in this rather posh restaurant. Following that, we were on our own. Always appreciating the chance for an evening swim before bed, I headed to the pool. There I met Lorien. He was seated in the corner of the room, clearly displaying a broad smile while enjoying the laughter of several children and their parents. Such gaiety I too always found desirable as we were in an industry plagued by excessive complaints. No one ever seemed satisfied. Laughter was always the best tonic for the weary office worker.

During the conversation he encroached upon business. I didn't mind. He asked me about wrongful dismissal litigation and what I thought about his case. His client was a cleaner with a native casino who thoroughly enjoyed his job although most aspects of it were rather bland. Then the provincial government moved in taking control of the native casino, and Lorien's client lost his job.

The native community objected to the dismissal of its tribal member. It was just too abrupt. "Two weeks' notice," the pink slip said. However, in spite of the prospect of any sense, he was ushered to the door with just enough time to grab his cloak. He did receive the semi-monthly pay but that was it. He had no benefits and no medical plan. He was destitute. The reserve assisted as much as it could, concluding every meeting with expressions of enthusiasm. Paraphrased, they said, "Don't expect anything more." Lorien believed the chief had worked out a lucrative deal to benefit members of his council. He admitted he couldn't prove it, but determinedly noted that he couldn't understand the lack of effort by tribal council to protect the native jobs or why it just handed such a lucrative enterprise over to the government.

We spoke about this and other matters, ending with my pledge to request the advice from one of our firm's lawyers. They spoke the next morning before the conference reconvened. During a break, Lorien expressed his sincere gratitude and we once again exchanged business cards.

Four months later, in early February of 2006, Lorien called me. I was surprised, but felt very honoured that he would respect my knowledge and ability enough to ask for advice. His request was sincere because he was being twisted in circles by the experts and disputing lawyers. This always happens: exaggerating information with various concepts and possibilities to further the interest of one's client. However, in this case, he was confronting aspects that were hastily becoming brick walls.

Lorien's client, a native from his local community, had been asked by a former associate to assist at a project in a native community in rural Vermont. He was a welder by trade, but had skills in masonry work, particularly foundations. He also possessed the skill to operate a backhoe and other equipment. His client, because of the shortage of motel accommodation, was forced to stay in a rented trailer. That unit was equipped with a sizable water tank, and a generator. Meals were cooked on a kerosene-stove outside under a canopy. One night in the late fall of 2003, while he was sleeping, the trailer exploded. Lorien's client was rushed to hospital with second degree burns.

The hospital and medical bills in the States were extensive. Being a native from Ontario visiting Vermont, he didn't have any medical coverage. After much haggling, the provincial health plan did pick up the tab for the hospital bill. However, the cost of continuing care was becoming outrageous with the additional expense of increasing interest. There was no workers' compensation coverage.

Lorien's concerns involved both quantum and liability. How much was his claim worth for pain and suffering and future income loss? Which experts should he use? Who would pay for them?

With respect to liability, he had a much more pressing issue. Vermont at the time was not a 'contributory negligence state'. That meant that, in such circumstances, Lorien could sue and/or collect from only one person or firm. If that person or firm was liable then they could then sue others. The complex issue would drive most lawyers to avoid such cases.

Also concerning liability, the evidence was destroyed in the fire, and there was no subsequent inspection of the remains to suggest a potential cause.

Regarding all of these matters, one of our lawyers before coming to our office had dealt with similar issues in Vermont.

My response to Lorien was basically a series of questions asking about the medical and employment status of his client, the actions and support of his tribal council, the names of all parties in Vermont, and the identity of the manufacturer and supplier of the trailer, the stove and the generator. Perhaps the next question bothered Lorien most of all: "Who's the local judge?" Relative to the political sentiments in that county, the next query was automatic: "How does he feel about the aboriginal community?" The potential in the States to choose your preferred jurisdiction had to be considered.

The failure to preserve evidence was a key aspect in the entire case. Lorien believed the distributor of the trailer arrived on scene very quickly to remove the damaged trailer. With it he took the damaged generator and kerosene stove. That was his principal defendant. Our advice was to sue everyone involved in the manufacturing, sale and ownership of the trailer and then let the courts decide. No doubt the tribal band and the project coordinator would ultimately be involved.

Because the incident involved an event in Vermont with resulting treatment in Ontario, Lorien was dutifully advised to maintain legal action in both venues. He had already done that, but once again he appreciated the concurrence with his actions.

Fortunately, Lorien's client had filed tax returns in Ontario, even though his native status did not require him to do so. That would be most beneficial in proving a significant income loss as his past records, we were told, confirmed a regular stream of income that could be extrapolated into the future.

The next morning I emailed Lorien, sending him a list of medical experts in his area. I had talked to several of these care providers before sending the email, just to make sure that they were all on board and did not anticipate immediate payment for their efforts and reports. Lorien's gratitude was immense. Three years later the case was settled.

Before that case was resolved, Lorien called our office once again. His concern was harassment. "Why are natives always blamed whenever the police find a burned vehicle?" With the major recession preparing to devastate the economic lives of many communities, the tendency to commit crimes for petty gains was becoming too common.

Not everyone was rich enough to lose their shirts in Ponzi schemes. Theft from offices, warehouses, salvage yards, and even pharmacies were no longer front page news. Residential burglaries also became the quick fix for many impoverished persons trying to make ends meet or purchase tomorrow's narcotics. It was all about the need for quick cash.

However, the $1,000 antique could no longer be fenced for even $100. The era of stolen car phones and auto radios had long vanished. Meanwhile the automobile maintained its desirable value among thieves.

Lorien's concern remained very real. "Why are natives always being accused of stealing and torching cars?" The accusation didn't make sense. If someone wanted to profit from a theft, why destroy the goods that he could fence? Conversely, if a native stole a vehicle why would he ever burn the vehicle in his own front yard?

Unfortunately there was nothing we could do to help Lorien. His issue was determined by preconceived notions in society. As cruel as it was, the perception that Indians are prone to commit major crimes including theft and arson of a white man's vehicle was commonplace and seemed quite acceptable in the infantile minds that decided that the white man was cultured and the native was not.

Following the settlement of his Vermont case, Lorien called our office once again, not just to express his gratitude but rather to pose another query. It was obvious that his clients could never be stereotyped. This query was legitimate on an issue that is taxing to so many lawyers and which judges are hard press to determine with any reliability.

Lorien's client was a woman who operated a business with a store on the reserve and also by internet. The latter included clients throughout North America and several firms in Europe. Her family—mainly her daughters—were also involved in the family's agricultural enterprise in Mexico. The products that she sold in her store and by internet involved: oil paintings, wax candles and decorations, reproduction of native artifacts, wood carvings, and artistic reproductions of ancient maps. Her skill was first class.

Unfortunately, the woman was convinced sad times would never happen. She never filed tax returns, so it was going to be hard to establish a future wage claim with some reliability. To her benefit, though, she had records of her expenses relative to her enterprise in Mexico. The latter she had to complete to file tax returns there. It was the Mexican agricultural produce that saved her claim. The woman had always thought of herself as being very thorough. Regretfully reality proved her not to be so. Then again fate smiled when a link to the website governing the Mexican business produced invoices for the supplies relative to her domestic business. All of that was not possible without our office's direct intervention. Accountants had, to that time, avoided participation in the claim as they were prone to do when an aboriginal person was involved who had not filed complete tax forms and lacked supporting documents. Even with the ledgers we found, obtaining the service of an accountant proved to be impossible.

It took a visit to his office, and weeks in ours assembling all of the documents, recopying same, and then in one office assembling them all by date. We then talked to the suppliers who all admitted none of their accounts were in arrears. We then emailed the buyers in Europe. With statistics produced by the provincial government on the average income and profit margins from similar enterprises, we were able to start piecing together the various aspects and ingredients that would formulate her income loss.

Ultimately we did a comparison of her annual expenses and noted a 23% increase in those expenses following the accident. That 23% was a definite loss figure. Based on her available capital to purchase new supplies, we were able to reasonably conjecture a profit margin. It was less than what it should have been but certainly within reasonable expectations. That term 'reasonable expectations' was always difficult for any side in any litigation process to adequately confront. Any projection that avoids gross exaggeration could be deemed to be somewhat reasonable. We went a step further comparing the increase in costs on a yearly basis so that we could then assume the same annual increases for her sales.

The woman was severely scarred as a result of the motor vehicle accident. Her need for ongoing dental work would continue for years. A minor brain injury was diagnosed. Psychologically, she was a mess. Being defaced was hell for this previously successful woman. She went into a shell. Her daughters left permanently to work full time in Mexico. They had had enough of their mother's outrageous outbursts. Her husband too bolted the scene. Her life had collapsed.

Lorien achieved an excellent result, using the mediation process to finalize the settlement. His gratitude was overtly expressive.

We met one time after that. The evening conversation over supper was far more serious and reflective. Although he was native by birth in Moosonee, and having worked almost exclusively for the aboriginal community, he admitted he was worried about the future of some First Nations. "You can't dance and drum forever." Lorien was devoted to the total campaign to preserve native culture, but was becoming concerned by the vocal few whose suggestions were being misinterpreted as dogma as if such activities were solely the foundation of the aboriginal community.

Repeatedly in that conversation Lorien stressed health, education, support for seniors and jobs. "Why do we import goods from China, when we can make them here?" The 'here' to which he referred were the native communities. He added, "Pay our people a reasonable wage to make the products we import from China. The more you pay our workers, the less you hand out as social welfare to the chiefs and their counsel."

Lorien further added that he felt that even those with tribal cards should file tax returns and then be eligible to receive the better benefits available to Canadians off the reserve. So much of what he said made sense. "We must put an end to separate standards and conditions for education and health care."

He had my agreement.

When asked if he would ever contemplate the position of chief, he spoke candidly. "Never. It's a thankless job. Look at them. They all try hard, but they are stuck in the middle of a whirlpool. The federal government withholds funds, the provincial government waffles, and residents can never be satisfied with the conditions that bind them to poverty without human expectations."

The conversation expanded beyond provincial matters to include issues pertinent to the east coast. In particular, we spoke at length about the dispute regarding fishing rights in New Brunswick. Lorien was well-versed on the subject, which led me to suggest that he should join their legal team. He politely replied that he had already considered it.

As he had to be up early the next morning, we concluded our meeting by once again expressing mutual appreciation. We bid goodbye that day with a promise to never end our struggles for an improved quality of life for all Canadians.

Two months later redundancy claimed my position. Meanwhile Lorien continues to surpass clients' expectations.

2015

PASCAL

"Never enough." The words were scrawled in large script on the single page. Placed uniquely in the centre of the coarse wooded desk, the message was abundantly clear. Remnants of other projects were strewn in a manner reflecting forgotten importance. In many respects it truly symbolized the entire room and unfortunately the remainder of his dying days.

Retirement years had done me well. After being forced into that situation by workplace redundancy more than four years prior, I explored various activities to fill my days. Ever mindful that we are never able to add a moment to our life's span, the keen desire was to contribute in some deliberate way to help someone. The uncertainty of life and death had already followed me daily in the handling of tens of thousands of claims for people I would never meet again. Retirement years were just an extrapolation of that training, this time giving me the chance to assist others without having to report to any supervisor on how and what I accomplished. "The Golden Years" are always good for that. No supervision.

This visit to that retirement home in the last week of August was not my first. There had been two other elderly patients that I had already been visiting on a weekly basis. Spending time with the infirm is not difficult. What makes the process trying is the reality that each person still has family. Where are they? In spite of that dismay, I persevered until the time had come for each person to rest eternally.

Outside the building I toured the gardens. The entire realm provided an extraordinary release from the tensions of the daily world. The gardens were amass with arrangements of black-eyed susans, echinacea, geraniums, chrysanthemums, begonias and roses. The trees provided pinnacles skyward to heaven as well as broad shelter beneath their spreading bows. Fruit trees especially created a sense of fulfilment with apples, pears, plums and nectarines. On the incline beyond the far fence, golden wheat swayed with the breeze creating an immaculate contrast with the shades of green and floral displays. Within the grounds there was a stream that was diverted into several tributaries. Across each, ornate wooden bridges provided access. A series of Christian statues, and shrines revering the symbols of Hindu, Jewish and Muslim faiths affirmed ecumenical grandeur.

Rose greeted me at the front desk. She was totally inspiring in appearance and courtesy. Her light complexion had been tanned by the late summer sun. Brown hair was thick and tied in a bun to not hinder her chores. Her smile above all else was captivating. It was so rare to find anyone in that position to appear so enthusiastic.

The introduction was longer than usual as this particular patient had not had any other visitors. I had to explain my interest, the source of the referral, and my expectations. She promised me she could give me more information about the infirm person, but only if he signed the authorization.

That process seemed somewhat strange to me, as I was told that he had developed Alzheimer's and may not want to see me. Did he have the capacity to even know what he was signing? Was I just wasting my time?

After waiting in the lobby for more than ten minutes she returned with the signed sheets, keeping them neatly within her file. That dossier also included my resume and notes she had taken after reviewing the medical reports. The patient had been referred to this residence by his family doctor in Midland.

"He may not say much," she advised before providing any details of the patient's life. Her advice after that was a series of short comments.

Pascal was his name. He was in his seventies. That meant he was born before the end of the war. He was born near Belleville, a home birth in a native community. Rose stressed that. Upon hearing the information I immediately concluded that the home birth took place as they generally did in the reserves in order to avoid the hospital. Once there were hospital records, the name and age of the child were public records so that it would be impossible for a child to avoid a Residential School.

"He worked in Toronto." That intrigued me. "On the sky-scrapers," she continued. "After that he worked with the missions helping others."

"The Victor Mission?" I enquired.

"No. The army centre," she added referring to the Salvation Army hospice.

Rose mentioned that the doctor believed he also helped with legal aid cases, and eventually headed north to Midland. There he struggled to make ends meet while doing whatever he could in the native community.

"Probably why he calls himself 'Huron'." That stopped me instantly, as the last person in the Huron Nation had died years before. "It seems to have given him purpose," she added.

Enquiries, regarding his Alzheimer's, provided inconsistent answers. At one point I mentioned dementia and was abruptly corrected. Regarding doctors, there were none currently being seen, just medication to control the affects. Speech and concentration were significantly compromised. "He's worse late in the day." Her summary was consistent with other such cases.

Any questions I may have had regarding the care and commitment were immediately dispelled when I was informed that he had no medical plan, and no funds. "They basically took him off the street." That this residence and care were all 'pro bono' astounded and inspired me. In our computer age, when the whole world concentrates exclusively on input and output, it was a blessing to encounter a niche where humanity counted.

Rose led me upstairs to the second-floor room. Pascal had fallen asleep, huddled under his blankets facing the wall. "Always needs two covers," she advised. His heavy breathing clearly conveyed he was in another world. "Doesn't snore," she added, "just breathes hard even when he's up."

The comments led me to conjecture that maybe there were other issues. However, who was I to judge. So often with my own clients in the past there was a general reluctance to ever tell any doctor the complete story. That could have been the case here. Rose then left me alone in the room. "He should be up by four" was her parting expression.

I followed her out of the room and proceeded to the gardens. They reminded me so much of St. Bernard's Convalescent Hospital in North York. However, here, the technology was much more enhanced. As one neared a particular statue, a hymn could be heard. The statue of the Sacred Heart intrigued me. It was so much a copy of the one at the Carmelite Abbey in Niagara Falls. "Wonder if it was the same artisan." The thought was automatic.

At 3:30PM I was back in his room; Pascal had just awoken. My entrance startled him and his first impulse was to press his buzzer for security. I introduced myself. He didn't seem to understand, so I repeated the information. "Do you want me to open the window?" That question broke the ice. He just nodded and smiled. The breeze was instantly refreshing, filling the room with a fragrance. Considering all of the visits I had ever made, I always found fresh air to spark up a conversation. It did so this time.

Pascal looked very much his age. His wrinkled complexion could hardly be noticed under the forest of wiry hairs most men would call beards. There was no structure to the matted hair that continued up his sideburns and into the course thick locks that covered his temples and ears.

"Do you have a bowl?"

Either he chose not to answer or had difficulty with the words.

I left, and after a brief search returned with a bowl of soapy water, a face cloth and a towel. Thirty minutes later, the dirt in his hair was cleansed and his chin was shaved. Tomorrow, I pledged to myself, I would wash his hair again with better water and appropriate shampoo.

Queries about his past met with silence initially. Only after he figured I was a friend did he open up. However, his speech was rattled, most of the time just incoherent mumbling. I sensed that maybe he had spent too many hours in bed, which had caused phlegm to build up in his throat. The offer to take him outside initially met with his reluctance. In reply to the second offer, he mentioned supper. When I suggested we would be back for supper, he started to pull back the covers.

Pascal was a trifle annoyed when I did not hand him his dressing gown. Instead I told him to remove his pajama top and put on a t-shirt that I pulled from the closet. Outside, his steps were timid. He relied on a cane. We had used a wheelchair until then. Perhaps he quickly learned that he was not going to be the boss. We didn't walk long, only about fifty feet. Fortunately a park bench was there waiting for him. At that point the stream was flowing over a few rocks, creating the recurring splash of rolling whitecaps.

Supper was a trying event. I let Pascal win that time to ensure our friendship. He had had troubles talking and encountered even more difficulty feeding himself. Coordination was just not his specialty. Perhaps he was embarrassed in the cafeteria with others. Pascal, I believe, deplored the idea that he needed special treatment, and thus chose to never eat by himself in his room.

The few minutes after the meal in his room were an inconvenient silence. He was obviously tired and the effect of the Parkinson's, dementia or Alzheimer's was taking substantial control. He closed his eyes, this time with just one blanket covering him. The window was only slightly open enough to provide a hint of fresh air without substantially dropping the room's temperature.

In the quiet with only the hallway light, I checked the array of items on his desk. Interest was not just with that piece of paper with the key phrase 'Never enough'. So much can be learned by what is displayed and what maybe missing. What struck me immediately was the absence of any family photos. Similarly there was no wallet, no watch and no identity cards. There were small pages torn out of a pamphlet used to record telephone numbers. Most were just scribble. Pictures were drawn on two of the pages. They seemed to have been attempts at a native longhouse.

Before leaving, I bent over the old man already fast asleep. "Your mother loves you. Your father loves you. God bless and keep you."

Rose, unknown to me, stood in the doorway watching. She just smiled when I noticed her. Outside his room we spoke for just more than a minute until the murmur started. Surprise was instant. Then it got louder, repeating itself. Within a minute there was some coherence to the melody. "He does this every night."

Pascal was humming the remarkable and endearing tune by Gordon Lightfoot, "The Last Time I Saw Her Face." I couldn't believe it. Here was a man having considerable difficulty with his speech yet being able to hum a tune without any pause. Then my amazement became surprised shock as Pascal applied soft lyrics to the melody.

I looked in the room, ready to cry. That was not possible for a man diagnosed with Alzheimer's. Or was it?

"Did he tell you about Al?" Rose's question was quiet and to the point. "Ask him tomorrow," she prompted.

I couldn't say no.

The next morning, Rose greeted everyone wearing a bright green sleeveless dress. She was the spring of youthful enthusiasm. Instantly she advised that Pascal was awake waiting for me. That in turn raised my spirit of accomplishment.

Attendants had already helped him with his shower and changed his bedding. Pascal was seated in his chair looking out the window when I arrived. His smile was a polite acknowledgement, more than I had received the first day. After placing my bag on the table he asked if we could go outside. With the promise that we could do so later, I pulled out of my bag a bowl with four bottles of water, some shampoo, a face cloth and a towel. Although he complained as any old man would, Pascal's hair was washed. A shave followed and he was most presentable, no longer the old destitute reject that greeted me that first day. Others in the garden noted the improvement, and suddenly there were more smiles, warm salutations, and expressions of kindness from others that had never spoken to him or even acknowledged his presence in his first two weeks there.

For whatever reason, I really couldn't imagine why, I started humming a song from Crosby, Stills and Nash, "Teach Your Children". He knew the words. It was obvious that when it came to music his ability with lyrics surpassed his regular speech. The Beatles' "All You Need is Love" followed with Pascal being very deliberate on the refrain. From a distance, Rose and the others witnessed how music can revitalize a person.

We continued for more than an hour, seated on that bench beside the pear tree. At one point I asked him about playing cards or checkers. He shook his head and mumbled that he wasn't interested. He then checked himself and advised with a touch of difficulty, "Maybe later." Appropriately, I returned to the music with "I Like It" by Gerry and the Pacemakers. He was delighted. We continued to enjoy songs until lunch time.

In the afternoon, conversation again attempted to ascertain some information about his family. Silence was his answer. Rose had said he would never talk about them. Pascal proved her right. Before supper, I left him in his room. I had never asked about Al simply because I forgot. Plus I didn't remember the name.

Three days passed before I arrived again. Rose greeted me with news that Pascal may have a sister but she had no other information regarding her. "Maybe Midland," she conjectured.

My question about Al prompted her advice. Rose didn't know exactly who Al was but sensed he was very important to him. It was worth a try.

Rather than talking about Al or anyone else, we went outside. He finally allowed himself to play checkers although he told me he definitely hated the game. We hummed some tunes from the 1960s as that era was common to both of us. I added many of the lyrics. Pascal attempted his best to maintain the melody. I let him win the game of checkers to discern his capacity to think and plan the next move. It was now the seventh day of September.

The trip to Midland was eventful. With signed authorizations I met with the family doctor while he was on duty at the hospital and with the police, and then visited the Little Huron Village within the city. The family doctor remembered the name 'Christine' who he believed lived in Sutton. The police knew of

Pascal as several times a few years ago they had picked him off the street during inclement weather. The curator of the village remembered Pascal, not by name but by his appearance and the fact he kept on asking for work. When I enquired if there was any prospect of Pascal's relationship to the Huron Tribe, his answer was direct: "He definitely claimed to have some distant relation. I don't know who, but he was very definite."

The next morning I telephoned the doctor's office to verify any information on Pascal's parents. His note indicated that at the time of his first visit the clinic was told they were deceased.

A trip to Sutton that same day generated nothing productive. There were many persons named Christine in the municipal records. However, for each there was no indication of age. The Vernon Directory similarly was inconclusive.

The next time I met Pascal, while we were outside wearing our jackets, I asked him about Christine. His scowl told me to keep quiet. I insisted, telling him this retirement home could not keep him indefinitely and that I had to meet with her to finance his stay. He looked to the ground ignoring me. I insisted. He then became angry and incoherent. We had to return to his room.

There I tried to apologize, saying I didn't want to make him angry. He just looked away, staring out the window to some phantom presence. I stayed, remaining quiet. Pascal obviously didn't want me there. After more than five minutes I stood up and approached his desk. Without asking his permission I started to sort papers. It was a vindictive stare but he said nothing.

Several papers and scribbled notes I checked closely. Further inspection was definitely required. These I eased to the side, planning to review them at home.

There was a set of keys in one drawer but no identity tag. "Your home on Main Street?" Hopefully the ambiguous question would prompt him to talk. His silence continued.

In the back of the lower drawer a photograph and several prayer cards were discovered. Two of the laminated cards presented the image of Blessed Kateri. The other one highlighted the Canadian Martyrs. On its reverse side there was the usual

Novena Prayer. I placed these three on his bedside table. The photograph was creased with its corners cut. The picture of a green parrot was inconsequential.

After leaving the room, I went downstairs to meet with Rose. Explaining the situation, I advised that Pascal was obviously Catholic. She called the local parish and asked for a pastoral visit.

In his room, Pascal smiled upon receiving advice that a priest would attend. After supper we spent time together, just talking. As long as I didn't ask about his family, the conversation flowed as if it were between close friends. He still had difficulty at times pronouncing certain words. Forgetfulness increased as it always did late in the day. Even when he had to say things three times, courtesy demanded a smile in response.

Before 8PM, he had closed his eyes and was drowsing off to sleep under the comfort of two blankets. As was the norm whenever I was there that late, I stayed for a moment outside his room to hear a tune he would instinctively hum. He answered my expectation as if a song each night carried him into his dream world where there was no pain, no sorrow, no tribulation.

The melody of the religious song "Be Not Afraid" grabbed my heart. As slowly as he carried the tune, equally deliberate were his words. He knew them by heart. My thoughts reacted with a sense of dread. This song was normally sung during a funeral procession leaving the church. What did it all mean?

You shall cross the barren desert, but you shall not die of thirst.
You shall wander far in safety though you do not know the way.
You shall speak your words in foreign lands, and all will understand.
You shall see the Face of God and live.

Rose, who had been standing in the hall, tried to calm my reaction. She confessed that she had heard those lyrics before, describing his ritual as his means of "Being at peace." She then praised him, stating emphatically that "I've never met anyone like him."

Emotionally I was exhausted by the time I arrived home. Based on that melody, would I ever see Pascal again?

The next morning came quickly. Rose was all smiles in those early hours. "Did you ask him about Al? Oh yes, the priest is coming today."

As soon as the name was mentioned, Pascal informed me that Al was a 'she'. Perhaps the full name was Alicia or Alice or Alexa. In any event, it seemed strange for a bird, not just any bird but Pascal's conure.

Research was not required to determine how intelligent those birds were. Pascal told me everything I had to know or in his mind that I should know. "Like having a two-year-old child who never grows up" was his summation. Pascal's conversation, like his musical lyrics, improved immensely once he started talking about Al. Unfortunately he always referred to her in the past. That was unavoidable, as I quickly learned she had passed away on the 14TH of August, less than a month ago.

His litany of her accomplishments and daily routine had me mesmerized. Birds were birds, weren't they? How could any breed be so different?

"The first day I got her, I was lying on the floor against the couch watching TV. She got off the table and climbed on me. Then she walked to my face, stared into my eyes, pressed her beak against the side of my nose and fell asleep."

At the time Al first entered his life, he lived in a three-room apartment. Pascal started releasing information about his own past, only when it related to his years with Al.

She had her cage but rarely stayed inside. Being well-trained, she had papers around the cage and dutifully made her deposits there. Al had her own stuffed animals and could look outside a window into the garden when Pascal was not home. In that garden she adored the opportunity to sit on her favourite branch in the pear tree. Other birds would perch in the same tree and sometimes even on the same branch. Pascal admitted he discovered the wonderful tendency among the birds to stay committed to mates for life, and in spite of what nature books told us, that there was a camaraderie among different breeds whenever a feathered creature was in need. Clearly they had attributes that humans had abandoned.

Al's breakfast always included a small portion of a slice of cold meat, and a piece of apple, pear, peach or orange—whatever was in season. Similarly, raspberries and blueberries were considered a morning delicacy. There were of course her seeds, and always a crust of his toast. If ever his supper included a portion of meat, she went crazy for the bone. Chicken was her favourite. Who said birds are not carnivores?

That friendship with his best friend ended when he lost his job during the Great Recession. Pascal was near tears as he related how he had to give her up because he could no longer afford his own place. Then, in 2011, having found employment with a landscaping firm that also majored in snow plowing contracts in winter, he was able to rent an apartment and provide a home for his loved one.

Al was accustomed to walking from one room to the next. Flying indoors was no longer required. She'd have her baths in the sink. Each evening she'd be on his shoulder while he watched television or listened to music. Every night they would sleep in the same bed, with Al either on top or below her own pillow. A car ride for coffee or donuts was a daily treat. He'd take Al to the local playground to see the children. The bird enjoyed laughter. She would never fly away. Occasionally she'd taunt the dogs knowing Pascal would protect her. In the event she suddenly got scared she'd cuddle up to him or scurry under his sweater. This was a true love affair oft recorded in Hollywood epics. There had never been another small bird that made so many people smile.

For three days his stories captivated us—not just myself but others as we sat outside under the pear tree. I realized why Pascal came to life under the branches of that fruit tree. It reminded him so much of a little creature.

Then it all suddenly happened. Early in the morning of the 14TH, his lifelong friend passed away in his hands. Pascal buried her underneath a tree in the park where she had entertained so many children. That had been her home away from home.

That same day everything changed. Pascal once more added details concerning his ailment. He had functioned for some time being able to maintain his job due to the kindness and compassion of his employer. Heavy machinery was out of the question. However, still being able to rake, move plants, or just sweep— he remained a valuable employee.

Once Al died his life fell apart. Within three days an ambulance attended. Tests, particularly the MRI, revealed major issues. His family doctor and neurologist completed the forms. Pascal then found himself dispatched to this home on an emergency basis.

In his stories, several times he referred to his life with Al as being "Heaven on earth." I understood that clearly from his devotion. "Is she in heaven?" It was a question I had never contemplated before, but I assured him Al was.

Pascal had been able to hide his tears quite well that day. Usually narratives about his friend caused an emotional outburst compelling me to take him back to his room. It had been a long day. He had made many more friends with his detailed narratives. Pascal had generated the smiles that he knew Al would if she was still present. But was she present?

In the drawer next to his bed someone had placed a sheet of beige coloured paper with this prayer.

My dearest family,

    Some things I'd like to say, but first of all, to let you know that I arrived okay. I'm writing this from heaven.

    Here I dwell with God above. Here there's no tears, only love. I am still with you. Please do not be unhappy because I am out of sight. Remember that I am still with you every morning, noon and night.

    That day I had to leave you when my life on earth was through, God picked me up, hugged me, and said, "I welcome you."

    God gave me a list of things to do, and first on that list was to watch and care for you. When you lie in bed at night, and the day's chores are put to flight, God and I are closest to you in the middle of the night.

When you think of my life on earth and all those loving years, because you are human they are bound to bring you tears. But do not be afraid to cry, it does relieve the pain. Remember there'll be no flowers unless there was some rain.

I wish I could tell you all that God has planned. But if I were to tell you, you wouldn't understand. But one thing is for certain, though my life on earth is over, I'm closer to you now than I ever was before.

Rose was adamant that she did not know it was there, repeatedly telling me that Pascal never displayed any inclination to value any keepsake. It was as if he had surrendered all hope the moment that Al died in his hands.

I called his family doctor the next morning. He was not available but the medical assistant was quite informative. She agreed that she was amazed yet disturbed as to how Pascal had "fallen off the edge once his friend had died." In truth, his demise was extremely quick. There was no doubt that Al was keeping his condition at bay, providing him with the inspiration to excel, to be overly positive in spite of inevitable degeneration, and to laugh and smile when there was no hope. The medical assistant thanked me and pledged to refer this issue to others especially any medical student wishing to engage in further research for his Masters or PhD.

My time with Pascal that morning was spent discussing his only real concern "Is Al in heaven?" Having expected that to be a topic of conversation, I already ordered Friar Wintz' novel 'I Will See You in Heaven'. The more I agreed with him, the simpler Pascal's life began.

When Pascal had sung the phrase, "cross the barren desert", was he referring to Al walking from one room to another to join Pascal on the couch? When Pascal had whispered the words, "speak your words in foreign lands", did he refer to the bird's ability to understand words and converse with more than fifty different chirps? When Pascal had pledged that Al will "see the Face of God and Live", he was at peace.

At home that night, my mind started to race. It wasn't just about the conure, or about Pascal's ailment.

Does a person have to own a tribal card in order to be aboriginal in practice or indigenous in thought?

Did Pascal's love affair with Al have anything to do with his native inclinations?

Was his homelessness or temporary destitute status attributable to any public perception of his aboriginal heritage?

The questions were many, and each answer automatically prompted further enquiries. The complex issues could and cannot and never will be addressed in one simple answer. That has always been the fallacy of our politically correct society. You just can't wish 'equality'. It takes commitment and prolonged effort, not just today but always.

Pascal's admiration and affection for his pet demonstrated the intricate aspects of caring when one wishes to share to the ultimate degree. It became so evident from his many stories that this gentleman cared so dearly not just for Al but for all of nature, to create a world of encompassing virtue where smiles replace threats and conflict, where children's laughter is more important than profits, where all sense of discrimination and difference are concealed in the grandeur of nature, and where quiet moments of affection echo the need to share. Pascal's kinship with Al was enhanced by his inherent native kinship with God's creation. We can all share that bounty.

Thus a tribal card is not required to think like a native or to be an indigenous person. We must all desire to make this world a profoundly better place and in doing so guarantee ourselves that we will share in an eternal abundance of grace. For what is 'grace' if it's not the presence of God?

That December was incredibly warm, too uncomfortable for many who had already donned their winter wear. For others, it was impeccably wonderful. The priest arranged his schedule to celebrate Christmas Mass on the afternoon of the 24TH, outside in ten degree Celsius weather. Families gathered around. Rose became engaged at Christmas. For Pascal, he had one visitor and longed for another.

It was late in January when he said good-bye to us. In heaven, Al had already established her perch in her favourite tree . . . waiting and knowing. Can you imagine the expression on their faces when they greeted each other?

So often we forget to thank the Creator for the opportunity to meet so many interesting people in our lifetime. Allow this moment then to express gratitude to all of these momentary guests in our lives. Let them become the solid pillars, the totem poles, of our future and of our society.

Sources

Narratives concerning the thirteen individuals in this novel coincide exactly with their advice, perceptions, expectations and information. Personal friendships and direct involvement provided the many opportunities to share their difficulties, dreams and achievements.

Besides the information from those direct sources, the author, in order to verify events, referred to the following texts and documents.

Acoose, Sharon, *A Fire Burns Within*, Vernon, BC: JCharlton Publishing, 2016, ISBN 9781926476117.

Archive of the Jesuits in Canada, website, 2016.

Barkwell, Lawrence et al, *Métis Legacy: Michif Culture, Heritage, and Folkways*, Saskatoon: Gabriel Dumont Institute, 2006. ISBN: 0920915809.

Canada Census, *Population by Selected Ethnic Origins, by Province and Territory*, 1971 to 2006.

Canadian Senate Standing Senate Committee on Aboriginal Peoples: "The People Who Own Themselves" Recognition of Métis Identity in Canada, 2014.

Catholic Independent Schools of British Columbia, website, 2012.

Chippewas of Rama First Nation, website, 2015.

City of Kamloops, website, 2016.

City of Thompson, Hub of the North, Municipal Publication, 2013.

City of Thompson, website, 2016.

Cree Nation of Chisasibi, website, 2006.

Curve Lake First Nation, website, 2012.

Davis, Stephen, *Mikmaq: Peoples of the Maritimes*, Halifax, NS: Nimbus Publishing, 1998. ISBN: 9781551091808.

Diocese of Kamloops, website, 2012.

Friesen, Gerald, *The Canadian Prairies*, Toronto: Toronto University Press. 1987. ISBN: 0802066488.

Grant, Bruce, *The Concise Encyclopedia of the American Indian*. New York: Wings Books, 2000. ISBN: 0517693100.

Hansen, John et al, *Urban Indigenous People*, Vernon, BC: JCharlton Publishing, 2015. ISBN: 9781926476056.

Josephy, Alvin, *500 Nations: An Illustrated History of North American Indians*, New York, New York: Alfred Knopf, 1994. ISBN: 0679429301.

Lockerby, E., *Ancient Mi'kmaq Customs: A Shaman's Revelations*, The Canadian Journal of Native Studies, Bear Paw Publishing, 2004. ISSN: 07153244.

Muckle, Robert, *Indigenous Peoples of North America: A Concise Anthropological Review*, Toronto: University of Toronto Press, 2012. ISBN: 9781442603561.

Neely, Sharlotte, *Native Nations*, Vernon, BC: JCharlton Publishing, 2014. ISBN: 9780991944194

Newfoundland and Labrador Heritage Website, internet, 2016.

Pentland, David, *Handbook of North American Indians, Vol 6*, p227. Washington DC: Smithsonian Institute, 1981.

Porter, Frank W., *The Coast Salish Peoples*, New York: Chelsea House Publishers, 1989. ISBN: 1555467016.

Proctor, Dorothy, *Chameleon: The lives of Dorothy Proctor*, Far Hills, New Jersey: New Horizon Press, 1994. ISBN: 9780882820996.

PTBO Canada, 13 *Historical Facts about Indigenous People*, Peterborough Canada, 2016.

Queens Printer for Ontario, *About Moosonee*. 2010.

Sabatini, Lawrence, *My Journey: Musings of a Missionary*, Chicago: Mary Brown, 2010. ISBN: 9780615346960.

Statistics Canada Census figures and demographics.

Suttles, Wayne, *Handbook of North American Indians, Vol. 7*, pp486-7. Washington: Smithsonian Institution. 1981.

Truth and Reconciliation Commission, Honouring the Truth, Reconciling the Future, Winnipeg. 2015.

Waldram, James, *As Long as the Rivers Run*, University of Manitoba Press, 1993. ISBN: 9780887556319.

ACKNOWLEDGEMENTS

Immense gratitude is expressed to these thirteen persons whose stories confirm all of the anxieties and tribulations experienced by Indigenous Persons who strive to succeed away from the comforts of their First Nation Communities.